Shadows and Fury

STRANGE TALES

Written and Illustrated

by

Alice Rhenna Lenkiewicz

ISBN 979-8-88940-169-8

Preface

In 1995, my life in Oxford underwent a significant change. Three years into my marriage and expecting my first child, I left behind my carefree solo adventures to embrace new responsibilities for my growing family.

During this time, I revisited the memories of the places and experiences that had captivated me, during my European journeys. My interest in folklore and surrealism grew as I travelled across America, especially in Santa Fe, New Mexico, where culture, magical realism, and art deeply influenced my creativity.

Back in England with my husband, our explorations in the Baltic States and Poland rekindled my passion for illustration and storytelling, inspiring the creation of this book.

In this book, you'll find stories that trace my journey from an adventurous spirit to the challenges of motherhood. These stories explore personal freedom, rebellion against societal norms, and the ongoing quest for individuality and self-discovery. Through these tales, I've blended elements of fiction and non-fiction to express the strong desire to break free from societal expectations and explore the uncharted territories within ourselves.

"Beware; for I am fearless and therefore powerful."
Mary Shelley

A Message from the Guardians of this Book

Close your eyes,
And let me tell you a frosty tale,
Across your enchanted mind.

I am a princess embraced by winter's cold,
A dweller beneath the gentle glow of the moon.
My home lies beneath the embrace of ice and snow,
I traverse realms of both joy and sorrow.

Excuse my pale, otherworldly appearance,
A witch's curse deprived me of what was rightfully mine.
Jealousy consumed her, you must understand,
For her lover's heart longed only for me.

Though conflict and chaos bring little joy,
The world has turned away from the pure light of truth,
In its misguided and wandering ways,
Yet glimpses of the icy realm guide us home.

The moon's shadow creates a protective shield,
Something you can grasp or wield.
But enough of these icy tales, listen closely,
Enter my palace, woven!
with the silver touch of the moon.

My essence shines, sparkling brightly,
My embrace opens to you this very night.
But do not betray me, or the sea will claim you,
Unseal the door and walk the icy path by the tree.

Contents

THE DANCE

In the garden, the air is abundant with the scent of blooming flowers, their bright colours and delicate petals reaching toward the sky. A spectre, with tattered wings, glides through the garden like a faint, long-forgotten dream. Her presence is more felt than seen, and her wings make a soft, fragile sound, a memory of a past friend, now preserved like a porcelain figurine.

When she takes flight, the garden seems to wither and disappear, leaving a sense of longing. But then, she reappears, emerging from the darkness like a ghostly figure. She shimmers in a hazy, beautiful way, and her voice, when she sings, is like a haunting melody from another world.

A mysterious map, like a strange, embroidered cloth, is filled with mysteries and secrets. It softly glows, revealing a path as intricate as a spider's web. The veil, crafted with great care, seems to hold ancient and unseen powers. It creates dancing and flickering shadows in the moonlight, creating a magical world.

The moon, a silent and wise observer, hovers in the sky, its gentle light touching the veil. Its followers, with their otherworldly presence, examine the fabric, making sure it sparkles with charm. The moon appears to have a special connection with the veil, and they interact like a celestial dance of light and shadow.

The sun, a warm and passionate presence, shares its desires, adding conflict to the celestial spectacle. It despises darkness and shadows, and its words are like intense heat. The moon's followers acknowledge the sun's warmth, and they all join in a captivating dance of shimmering rays in the night sky.

An enigmatic figure, shrouded in dark clothing, stands in this surreal scene. The map seems to ripple like a liquid dream, and an eerie glow surrounds the figure as shadows twist and turn in an otherworldly aura.

As the figure gazes at the mysterious map, uncertainty fills the air. The sun, as a guide, has abandoned its path, leaving the traveller with endless possibilities. Yet, the figure finds joy in this uncertainty, and with determination, it takes the first step on the ever-changing path. It leaves no trace as it walks on the fabric of a dream. The journey into the unknown begins, and the world becomes a tapestry of mysteries and enchantment, where riddles and secrets are waiting to be discovered.

SECRETS OF THE FOREST

Bonnie's life was a surrealist painting come to life, a soft, vague pink chiffon scarf that obliterated the stark, vivid colours of the world and immersed everything in a milky harmony. Whenever she wanted to see the world differently, she would don the scarf and peer through its hazy view, squinting her eyes and distorting what she didn't want to see, adding a tree here and taking a person away there, whatever felt better at the time.

The street she lived on never changed. It gathered the desert dust like a witch casting a spell, the golden sand blowing through the narrow town and then disappearing without a trace. It was as though it were secretly devoured by one of the decaying barns that had stood there for years, with only one haggard red gaping door and a white-washed facade that has worn away like an old face, slowly revealing one wrinkle after another.

That window, a sinister omen that hung precariously, about to collapse mirrored everyone who lived there. That was the crazy thing about that forsaken town; there was a desolation that seeped through every crevice of its existence. It symbolised a morbid evolution towards oblivion, where everything was waiting to die, the buildings, the flowers, the trees, even the people. If someone didn't die today, it was tomorrow, and you just sat waiting for your turn, until you went mad, and nothing mattered anymore. The people danced on the edge of a precipice, trapped within the cycle of inevitable demise.

Suddenly, you find yourself just living for the moment, until that old feeling returns, and you realise that nothing has changed, and nothing will get better. You dwell in this paradoxical moment, where the past and present merge into a mystified tapestry of existence, and the future remains an enigmatic puzzle.

Bonnie grappled with the enigma of time. She kept slinging plates of grub to a bunch of poker-faced customers, her mind drifting to a far–off haven of excitement, a place where dreams had a fighting chance. The daily grind had chewed her up and spat her out, one too many times. She craved a change, something that'd slap her senses awake. She started yearning for a taste of the unknown, a desire for something wild. She was going to take a leap of faith. Her eyes sparkled with excitement and with adventure on her mind, she left the town behind. It was time to dive headfirst into this crazy world.

She put her blonde hair in a chignon, put on some red lipstick and some kitten heels, tossed a few essentials into her suitcase and hit the road, the world stretching out before her like an exhilarating mystery.

Hours passed as she walked the unyielding path under her feet, unfurling like a riddle to be solved.
Eventually, she stumbled upon a small clearing bathed in the soft golden light of the setting sun. And there beneath the sprawling branches of an immense oak tree lay a handsome rogue of a man, smoking a cigarette who reminded her of a past lover she had left behind in the smoky nightclubs of Chicago.

As if it were completely natural, they suddenly found themselves in a curious and daring embrace. Then, without uttering a word, passion consumed them in that forgotten glade, under the watchful eyes of the ancient oak.

The world ceased to exist as two souls were burning with intensity. In the soothing shadows of the forest, they found solace in each other's company. As they lay together in harmony, Bonnie enquired about the man's occupation.

"I'm a crook," he admitted, the words saturated with the raw grit of his criminal life. His voice bore the heavy burden of a thousand secrets. "I'm here to shake down this forest."
Bonnie's heart raved, her intuition keen to the desperation she heard somewhere within his confession.
"Why are you turning to the woods, of all places?" she inquired, her curiosity edged with suspicion.
"Money, babe," he responded, the lines on his face, reflecting a sorrowful determination. "My family is on the line, and I've got to put food on the table, one way or another."

Bonnie couldn't help but feel a pang of compassion for him. It was a moment of understanding, an acknowledgement of the unforgiving circumstances that life often presented.

"I can assist you," she said quietly in the tranquil night. "I know the way into the deep forest."

The man's eyes softened with gratitude, a flicker of hope igniting within his weary gaze. "I appreciate that," he replied.

Within the maze of heavy thickets and winding trails, they ventured deep into the mysterious heart of the forest. The man, driven by a thirst for security and knowledge, aimed to uncover the hidden secrets that the forest guarded.

In the hushed gloom, Bonnie's footsteps led him to a fabled golden tree, its gnarled branches cloaked in a spectral luminescence. She parted the gilded foliage, unveiling a secret doorway, shimmering with an ethereal golden sheen. Stepping through the threshold, they traversed a realm where time seemed to waver, and the laws of reality blurred into an enigmatic dance.

As they emerged from the veiled passage, they found themselves standing in the heart of a haunted glade, where shadows blended with eerie sentience and the air hummed with the whispers of forgotten spirits.

In the profound twilight, Bonnie looked up transfixed by the shimmering stars, her pale slender arms outstretched as if to beckon the celestial, dance above. The stars cascaded like elusive embers upon her form, weaving an otherworldly tapestry of fleeting enchantment that embraced her being in a spell of ethereal allure.

Beside her stood the man, his grip on her slim waist, firm, yet tender, a silent witness to the interplay of light and shadow within the depths of his troubled soul.

During gentle whispers of remorse and the quest for self-understanding, he suddenly desired her, drawing her closer to him, seeking comfort in her presence. As her crimson fingernails clung to the tree, Bonnie felt like a deity, embracing a newfound surge of self-empowerment.
"Don't ever leave me," he commanded.
"I promise," she vowed, as the moonlight disrobed them in its opal sanctuary.

THE RED BRIDE

The bride, dressed in a fiery red gown, gazed into the mirror. Her pale skin, once caressed and touched, now seemed destined to remain untouched forever. She imagined herself frozen at this moment, forever wearing the red dress until her skin became wrinkled like tissue It was what was expected of her, after all.

Her past lovers resented her, accusing her of bitterness and negativity. But only she knew the truth. The truth was that she was now free, free to feel the smooth silk of her dress against her skin, free to imagine the perfect hand in hers. She felt as if she was on fire.

Gazing at her reflection, she could no longer see her husband or her past lovers. All she could see was a vast, green meadow, where she, the bride in her red dress, was free to explore and run.

She walks gently through forests, alongside sinuous lakes, and through glades that unveil glassy ponds. She appears to glide through these areas, her crimson dress fluttering amidst the trees akin to a gorgeous sunset. Occasionally, she encounters other brides, and they extend greetings to one another under the scorching sun, transmuting their pristine white dresses into white swans. The sun metamorphoses the trees into shimmering lanterns, and when the day culminates in its hottest moment, they all descend within boats and sail along the river.

They sail the river like spectres, everlastingly ablaze with desire. The sun singes the water into a profound violet hue, akin to some toxic treacle. When the heat intensifies, even the poisonous treacle appears alluring, and the brides descend into the water one by one. It feels comforting, and at that precise moment, they comprehend that they are finally experiencing something they do not typically feel—they can read each other's minds.

"Jump in, jump in," the brides called out, "it's so soothing and wonderful."

The bride did not. Instead, she changed direction and sailed the boat towards the sun until she became consumed by it, dissolving like a watercolour painting. The tones on the water shimmered in diluted columns, forming an abstract masterpiece.

The sky transitioned from red to orange to violet, saturating her dress as if she might be absorbed into the intense visual heat.

She knelt and ran her hand through the marbled water, each colour gracefully flowing into the next like a psychedelic pattern. The green pigment circled through the yellows, the blues, and the reds. When her hand emerged, it was covered in a veil of imaginary landscapes, creating a glove fit only for a woman inside a painting.

Frequently, she could be observed by the water's edge, patiently waiting until the distant lights dimmed as if an artist had gradually obscured each hue with black paint, leaving only the essential colour behind. In this instance, it was a subdued green glow, softened by the presence of the surrounding lights.

This was the light that always remained in the darkness on Simian's wooden boat, winking softly like a mermaid's sleepy eye.

The other brides glided through the twilight, the water reflecting their white gowns. The moon dangled like a luminous tear as they sailed toward it, into its obscurity, where the unborn await to enter the mysterious.

THE PRINCESS IN THE POND

Mother said, "Oh look at the moon. Isn't it beautiful?" We both looked up at its silver surface surrounded by glittering stars adorning the lush, ebony sky. Mother's face was lit up by the luminescence from above. I spoke but she didn't hear me as she was too captivated by the moon's spellbinding allure.

"Wouldn't it be nice if we could all live there," she sighed. "I would love to be young again. I mean I love being this age, but it would be wonderful to be appreciated for one's beauty and youth again."
"It's quite odd, isn't it?" I responded, "I never imagined I'd grow old, but here I am."

We felt quite drowsy. Eventually, Mother did drift into slumber. I gazed over the balcony. The trees were gently swaying and for a moment all the happiness that I could ever wish for coursed through me like an elixir.
"I can be anyone in the world that I want to be," I pondered ideas like flora adorned with feminine countenances, cats capable of transforming into humans, or butterflies with humanlike forms flitted through my thoughts.

While I contemplated these matters, my gaze descended beneath the balcony, directed toward the pond below. Submerged beneath the water's surface lay a princess with glorious golden hair, cascading like sunbeams. A serene smile graced her countenance and I noticed she wore a sapphire ring, its blue radiance dancing with an otherworldly charm.

Years after this incident, my mother told me that when she had divorced, she had thrown her wedding ring into the pond. "This is to freedom!" she had said assertively.
"No one will ever trap us again!" I replied.

However, as I observed the ring adorning my finger, an icy sensation coursed down my spine. I sensed that the princess dwelling within the pond yearned for my presence, her desire to pull me into the profound depths of the water, where I would remain for all eternity.

17

After many years, I looked back to this moment and began to wonder if my mother had been happy with her decision. After all, she had given up her marriage, her home, and her family. And for what? A life of freedom? But what did that even mean?

I remembered back to that night we had stood on the balcony, looking up at the moon. Mother had seemed so happy then. But was she? Or was she just trying to convince herself?

I don't know the answers to those questions. But I do know that I will never forget that night. It was the night that I realised that life is full of mysteries and that there are no easy answers.

THE FLOWER OF GOODNESS

Within a dreamscape, a benevolent bloom bares her petals to the heavens, her countenance encircled by an aura of purity. Swaying gracefully, her ethereal beauty stands in stark contrast to the frigid, rugged mountaintop upon which she finds herself.

Beneath her, a mass of twinkling lights resembles joyous forms, as the boundless expanse of the night sky engulfs her. Longing to be closer, she yearns to reach the celestial bodies above, beckoning her with their resplendent allure.

Teetering on the precipice, she stands on tiptoe, her heart a tumultuous blend of awe and trepidation. The icy gusts of wind whip around her, yet she remains captivated by the celestial spectacle above. The stars beckon her, their beauty enticing her to join them. However, hesitation grips her soul, for she comprehends that a misstep could result in an irrevocable fall, banishing her from the realm of flowers where she once danced joyously under the sun's warm embrace.

Days elapse, and she remains perched upon the mountaintop, paralysed by indecision. Finally, unable to resist the gravitational pull of the stars any longer, she takes a deep breath and surrenders to the void. As she plummets, her delicate petals drift away, each one a minuscule seed of hope. They disperse across the vast expanse of the sky, carried by the whims of the wind to distant lands.

19

Her fall seems endless, a never-ending spiral of pain and darkness. She can feel the wind whipping past her, tearing at her skin, and the ground rushing up to meet her. She knows that she is going to die, but she can't help but hope that she will survive.

Finally, she hits the ground with a sickening thud. She lies there motionless, her body bruised and battered. She can feel the blood seeping from her wounds, and she knows that she is dying. But even in her pain, she can't help but feel a sense of relief. She is finally free. She hears a sound. It is a faint, distant sound, but it is there.

She strains her ears to listen, and she realizes that it is the sound of music. It is the sound of the flowers weeping.

She opens her eyes and sees that she is surrounded by flowers. They are all different colours and shapes. She had never seen anything so beautiful. The flowers sing to her, and she feels their love and compassion. They tell her that she is not alone and that she is loved. They tell her that she is strong and that she will survive.

She believes them. She knows that she will survive. She knows that she will find a way to return. With a wriggle of her fingers and a flex of her legs, a surge of elation fills her being. Surveying her surroundings, she finds herself suddenly at peace and relaxing amidst a multitude of dandelions, their golden faces basking in the sunlight's warmth.

"Tell me the time," she inquires, and in unison, the dandelions respond, "It is the time to dance and the time to die. Join us, dear flower. Your time has come."
Embracing the invitation, she joins hands with the dandelions, and together they dance beneath the starlit sky. Their petals

and stems entwine, forming a harmonious unity, a symphony of life and death.

The following dawn, the field appears desolate, save for a multitude of torn green stems and diminutive dandelion clocks. They tick incessantly, awaiting the arrival of the next bloom to join them in their eternal dance.

She lies there for a moment, savouring the feeling of the sun on her skin. She can hear the birds singing and the bees buzzing.
She's acutely aware that this day will remain etched in her memory, the day when she narrowly escaped death and rediscovered her path towards her beloved sanctuary.

FAMILIAR PLACES

Pearly clouds and the sunbeam through the leaves like smiles. On the other side of the city, smog fills the carriage. A woman stands protecting her child from the pollution. What has happened to the laughter I wonder? The golden sun seeps through the sky and as dusk falls the colour changes to the dusky bitter colour of terracotta.

I look around this room. Gold and salmon pink with light green were once my choice of colours for this fireside. The enamel vase is displayed in a matching sequence. It reminds me of myself once; (an hourglass sprouting pink carnations). The vase is now as empty as I am. The life I once knew has now vanished.

Today, the town bustled with activity. The time-worn sunken church appeared as though it yearned for love, sinking further into the earth with each passing year, like a medieval princess laid to rest, in her tomb.

Today, a book on the enchantment of art serendipitously landed in my hands. It delved into the intricate geometric designs of timeless masterpieces and the analytical intricacies of snowflakes. These forms felt strangely familiar, floating before me like fragments of a mirror.
The skull, the horn, the papier-mâché, horse's head sit in their usual place. All these things that were once so meaningful now seem eerie and solemn.

The rain was so powerful today; clear and wild, as when I once had visions of melting into its prism waterfall. Houses stood solemnly with their granite facades and Victorian windows. Places where I once talked to those familiar faces are now gone and far away. The Christmas trees had somehow lost their vitality this year; they were not so sparkling or magical, not so proud. It was as if they had drawn their last breath.

The fire flickers and dances, its warmth enveloping me. I am alone, but I am not lonely. The people who once lived here are now gone, but their spirits linger. I am glad that I no longer live here, but I am grateful for the memories.

I hide away in my den, a place that exists outside of time. Here, the trees and the clouds are my companions. The wind whispers its secrets to me, and the fire tells me stories of the past. Today, something is different. I feel a strange sense of peace. I am content to sit here by the fire and watch the flames dance and flicker. I am content to be alone.

I close my eyes and take a deep breath. The smell of wood smoke and pine needles fills the room, and the sound of the crackling fire and the wind lulls me into a meditative state. I am one with the forest. I am the trees, the wind, and the fire. I am the earth, the sky, and the stars. I am all and nothing, and I am at peace.

THE THINGS WE DO FOR LOVE

In a shadowy and enigmatic realm, there stood a majestic tree. Its ebony branches reached high into the sky, entwined with the stars themselves, resembling a Georgia O'Keeffe painting. At the very top of the tree, nestled among the twinkling lights, was a radiant ruby jewel.

Deep within the jewel, a woman slumbered. She was a creature of extraordinary beauty, with long flowing hair, the colour of midnight and eyes that shone like precious gold. Her name was Anya, and she had been trapped by an evil entity within the jewel for centuries.

One day, a Viking prince named Bjorn was sailing through the skies in his magnificent ship. As he gazed among the stars, he noticed a glimmer of light that seemed to be calling to him. He followed the light to the tree and found Anya, sleeping within the ruby jewel.

Bjorn was immediately smitten with Anya. He vowed to rescue her from her prison, and so he began to climb the tree. The journey was long and perilous, but Bjorn was determined. Finally, he reached the top and without difficulty, he gently plucked the sparkling ruby jewel from its branch.

As soon as he did, Anya smiled at him and stepped joyfully out of the jewel and into Bjorn's arms. The two of them embraced, and between them, joy permeated the air.

Bjorn and Anya returned to Bjorn's kingdom, where they were married but their happiness was not to last. The evil witch named Morgana cast a spell on Anya, transforming her into a mermaid and thus trapping her forever in the deep ocean.

In the depths of his heartache, Bjorn wandered ceaselessly, seeking the elusive trace of Anya's presence. His desperate quest, spanning vast distances, proved fruitless, leaving him engulfed in despair. In a moment of profound anguish, he sought solace in the forbidden realm of dark enchantments.

He summoned a powerful demon and made a pact with it. The demon promised to help Bjorn find Anya, but only if Bjorn agreed to renounce his soul.
Bjorn had no choice but to agree, and the demon led him to the depths of the ocean, where he found Anya and freed her from a crystal cage.

Anya was overjoyed to be reunited with Bjorn, but she knew that their happiness would be short-lived. The demon had claimed Bjorn's soul, and he would soon come to collect it.

Bjorn and Anya spent their remaining days together, savouring every moment. When the demon finally came to claim Bjorn's soul, Anya was devastated. She begged the demon to take her instead, but the demon refused.

As Bjorn succumbed to the call of the underworld, Anya found herself drifting across the desolate expanse of the earth for countless years, plagued by solitude. Even her kin seized the chance to forsake her, subjecting her to cruelty and neglect. Their hearts turned frigid with envy, refusing to let her partake in their wealth, leaving her isolated and shunned.

One eerie day, Anya entered a mysterious forest that seemed to speak ancient secrets through its rustling leaves. In the center stood a dark cave, surrounded by sinister energy. Anya couldn't shake the uneasy feeling that inside the cave, the

demon who had stolen Bjorn's soul had found a wicked
sanctuary. The air felt tainted with the remnants of evil deeds,
and Anya sensed a foreboding presence.

Fueled by a sudden fearlessness and rage, she unleashed her
newfound strength to defeat the sinister force. The brutal
showdown saw Anya playing a slick game, fooling the demon
with bogus affection. Ultimately, she emerged as the
victorious warrior, her blade glistening with the vile blood of
the vanquished fiend.

With the liberation of Bjorn's soul, they were happily
reunited, returning to his kingdom where they lived happily
ever after.

CHINA FLOWERS

Once upon a time, there was a young maiden who lived in a
small village. She was a kind and gentle soul and found solace
in meandering through the bustling marketplace's crowded
stalls.

She would often admire the great mounds of embroidered
velvet and silk and dream of one day owning a chandelier
cascading with clear crystals.

One day, the maiden visited the market. She was feeling
weary and about to give up hope on her relationship. Things
hadn't worked out the way she planned. However, she saw a
delicate altar shining from a niche in the wall. The altar was
adorned with a statue, a broken mirror and religious milagros.
As her hand extended to touch the statue, a surge of profound

serenity overcame her and she knew she had found something very special, a feeling that enveloped her in otherworldly peace and tranquility.

The maiden continued to explore, and she found many other beautiful things such as resplendent Egyptian rings, bedecked with vivid gemstones, trailing necklaces reminiscent of cascading waterfalls, and intricately detailed china flower brooches, weaving an extravagant tapestry of opulence and an irresistibly exotic charm into her ensemble. She discovered a musical fountain, and she imagined the beautiful sensory experience of displaying this wonderous ornament in her garden.

The maiden revelled in her acquisitions, an air of anticipation enveloping her thoughts for the journey back home. Yet, an unforeseen impulse beckoned her towards the enigmatic allure of a nearby mansion, diverting her from her intended path. She slowly ascended the staircase, admiring the chandeliers, suspended from a giant profusion of pears and grapes in the heart of the ceiling. Upon entering the solemn red room, she ignited a candle.

The maiden stood there, her fingers trembling as they brushed against the china flowers adorning her dress. The distant sound of water flowing from the outside fountains merged with a feint unsettling musical chime. Memories of childhood summers in Cornwall flooded her mind but they were tainted by an overwhelming sense of foreboding.

Without warning, a searing pain pierced her finger. Startled, she glanced down to find the china flower shattered, her blood now shimmering red against her white dress.

An ominous dread consumed her very being. Panicked, she hastily fled the room, her footsteps echoing through the oppressive silence. She raced down the stairs, ran through the market and onto the sinister streets. She ran without looking back until she reached the safety of her home.

The maiden never forgot the strange house with the broken china flower. She knew that she had escaped something malevolent that day, the sensation of dread she experienced was etched into her psyche. As a result, she felt that her existence had been forever altered.

AUTUMN

I remember October and the red burning tree. A face gazed out at me engulfed in flames. The lads were building bonfires. The counsellors kept taking them away. One of the lads announced, "It's inside us, this pagan trait. We're just meant to burn wood!"

What was I thinking that morning? I was dreading work, but nothing mattered while the burning leaves surrounded me like a spiritual aura. The path was yellow, and violet, forming an iridescent glow. "I've had enough," I thought, "enough of it all." All those awful sour faces and tasteless rooms, people worrying and worrying, growing older and forgetting what it is like to be young. All I want is this avenue of yellow leaves, extended above me like a bountiful orchard of ripe yellow pears.

It was as though I was walking into a painting. Behind me, the bonfires blazed, and there lay the violet path from a tale of old. Everywhere around me, the world was painted in shades of gold and vermilion, adorned with hints of yellow,

28

ultramarine, and viridian green, yet overwhelmingly dominated by the enchanting presence of violet, violet, violet, with leaves aflame!

For a moment, it seemed three naked witches ran across the grass: their faces reflecting the miseries of life's fallen expectations. But under the golden trees, they suddenly become calm, like three carved pagan columns, standing still in the vibrant haze of dew and embellished trees. They stand there for centuries and at night they ignite like mystic torches, guiding the world towards enigmatic transformation.

The fiery red tree abided as a striking beacon in the October scenery, its branches reaching for the sky, resembling a maiden with her crimson hair, dancing in the wind. The leaves seemed to glow like embers in the transient rays of sunlight. It was a strange and beautiful sight to behold, entrancing me like a moth towards a luminous glow.

I approached the tree and gently ran my hand along its time-honoured bark. It was warm to the touch, and I could sense the warmth emanating from the flames. I closed my eyes and took a deep breath, inhaling the scent of the woods. It was a sweet and pungent smell, and it filled my head with strange and wonderful thoughts.

I opened my eyes and looked around. The world seemed different now as if I was seeing it through a new lens. The colours were brighter, and the sounds were sharper. I felt a sense of peace and tranquility that I had never sensed before.

I settled on the ground beside the tree and reclined. I shut my eyes and allowed nature to envelop me. I began to drift off into slumber, and soon, I found myself immersed in a peculiar and incredibly vivid dream. I was walking through the forest.

The trees were bare, and the ground was covered in snow. It was a cold and desolate place, and I felt lost and alone.

Suddenly, I saw a light in the distance. I walked towards the light, and I saw that it was coming from a small cottage. I knocked on the door. A very handsome man opened it. It was my best friend's husband. He was kind and welcoming, and he invited me inside. He gave me a cup of tea and we talked for hours. He told me about his life, and I told him about mine.

As my departure drew near, he gently unlatched the door and met my gaze. It was inevitable. Soon, we found ourselves locked in an embrace; our passion ignited by the crackling fire. He whispered that he had foreseen this conclusion, and later, as I bid farewell, he pressed a crystal into my hand, a token of protection. Feeling guilty at my lack of guilt, I left the cottage and continued my journey, still filled with thoughts of our unexpected encounter.

And then very suddenly and disappointedly, I awoke and realised it had all been a dream. Consequently, I experienced a profound sense of longing. The desire to return to the forest. My body quivered with longing and yet I was aware that it remained an impossibility.

Slowly, I rose to my feet and distanced myself from the fiery red tree. I acknowledged this place would forever remain fixed in my memory, and the recollection of my dream would always hold a special place in my heart.

ANOTHER DAY

Beneath the sun's radiant sky, the green waters shimmered like a tapestry of fragmented mirrors, evoking distant memories from my past. All around me, the world glistened in a bejeweled and vibrant green, a witness to the ageless crispness of time.

My thoughts found clarity and tranquility on this fine day, as a gentle breeze whispered to me and spoke, "Join us, ascend into the treetops where the fairies take flight!"

Oh, how I longed to reclaim my innocence, to witness the world anew. The cool embrace of the water soothed my weary feet during this searing July, and all around me, the earth bore the shimmering reflections of petals and blossoms.

Beneath the protective canopy of leaves, that warm breeze whispered in my ear, beckoning me, "Come join us, follow our guidance, embrace your youthful spirit, see the world in vibrant hues, and release your sorrows, and together we will achieve inner peace."

ICE

Ice breaks and the sky oozes droplets of chilling essence upon the ground, forming incisions in the frosted earth. All week the snow has concealed the branches of the trees; skimmed the surface of the rooves and hidden the view of my street allowing a few hazy lights to blink in the distance, through the midwinter sky.

The room feels cold amidst windows adorned with intricate frost designs, and I lose sensation in my fingers. I long for a cat to nuzzle in my lap, purring away, bringing warmth and comfort to my bitter hands.

Time to leave soon and behold new lands! I am young! Another life is waiting and beckoning patiently while I come to terms with the last residues of so-called refuge.

Perhaps I'm blindfolded. All along I've been blindfolded! Can one admit it? It appears isolation and death greet me once I leave. Can I, do it? Can I leave this secure cave and replace it with an opulent tree? Can I live with the sky and the birds hovering around me and observing me like vultures? Isn't that death? - when a bird has flown away from your tree and now it's observing you in the wilderness, all alone? Where to go? What to do? Should I crawl back to my cave? What awaits me on this callous evening? What will happen I wonder?

FROSTY MORNING

What a frosty morning it is. The sun's rays penetrate the shimmering grey mist, that drapes in the air like a shroud. The path beneath my feet is unyielding and unforgiving, and the trees that encircle it are barren and skeletal. I can hear the crisp crunch of my boots as they contact the icy soil.

I am not alone in my misery. Others are out and about, but they all seem to be hurrying to get somewhere. No one smiles or greets each other. The world has become an emptiness of faces in a myriad of despair.

The village is unobtrusive. The houses are obscure and silent, and the only sign of life is the occasional wisp of smoke levitating from a chimney and the woman wearing red stilettos, standing amidst the trees.

I shudder as I walk, prompting me to wrap my coat even more tightly around my body. The relentless cold penetrates deep into my bones, and I can sense my fingers and toes growing numb. I am not sure how much longer I can keep going.

Suddenly, I heard a sound. It is a piercing, high-pitched sound, and it seems to be coming from the woods. I stopped to listen. The noise is drawing nearer. I am afraid. I do not know what is making the sound. I turn and run, and I do not look back.

I ran until I couldn't anymore, and then I fell to the ground, panting heavily. My heart raced as I looked up and saw the woman with the red stilettoes looking down at me smirking. She placed her stiletto on my stomach. She takes a drag of her cigarette. I lie on the ground for a while, trying to catch my breath. The woman stands there, watching me as if I am a curiosity. Once I regain my strength, I rise and resume walking, quickly.

I walk for hours, and the sun is starting to set. I am tired and hungry, but I keep going. I stop to look around. The world seems so empty, so desolate. I feel a sudden chill run down my spine, and I shiver involuntarily. I am afraid, but I do not know what I am afraid of. I am tired but I cannot go home. There is no home for me.

I am solitary, with only solitude as my companion, a stark and unwavering presence in my desolate world.

BLISS

Where has the bliss flown to? Like dreams trapped within snowflakes, drifting throughout the night. Dissolving one by one, they have finally evaporated. I allowed them to flow above me like a waterfall, a spiritual catacomb.

Touch them! I wish I could touch them. This burden on my head is like a giant, brutal hand; if only I could run free, away from that hand; away from that obsession that will only be happy once it has swallowed and regurgitated me.

"It's alright," a soothing voice reassured me. I turned around and realized it was the one who held me, the closeness between us hinting at the possibility of a budding relationship, though we never broached the subject again. Suddenly, I thought I heard something and swiftly turned around. I could have sworn he said he loved me, but it was too late, he departed, fading away like a silent phantom of a lover.

One day I will escape my silent waterfall. Only then will I be able to see its emptiness as it once was, a crystal folly, situated like a phantom in the middle of that meadow.? That's when I'll be free and once again able to live in bliss!

35

CHANDELIERS

Chandeliers fall like tears. I think they are my tears, the kind that symbolises the transitions in my life, the shifts from girlhood to womanhood.

Looking up, I see the tears cascading towards me, a frozen waterfall in time. I could preserve my tears and attach them to the chandelier.

Not a single soul would discern the difference. Perhaps, with some spell or magic, I could conceal my tears every time sorrow overcame me and suspend them there. What if it happened in reverse? Picture the chandelier shattering, its crystals, transforming into tears, falling away from the ceiling. Amidst a lively dance, the revellers would suddenly find themselves surrounded by glass droplets, resembling mystical tears, scattered among the masked Venetian faces.

"Who is sad?" They would inquire curiously, but nothing would reveal the truth. They'd have to locate the crystal permanently affixed beneath my eye.

THE WOUND

The red horse with a woman's head trotted gracefully over the field, towards the lake. The sun blazed in the sky like a wound. Everything was red. Even her horse's body was red, galloping through a dreamscape, and then suddenly, another horse materialized.

This creature was a vivid shade of yellow, its large green eyes exuding a haunting presence that seemed to murmur melancholic memories. These eyes served as a portal to a nightmarish realm, invoking vivid recollections of brutal horse races, particularly that traumatic moment when she had tumbled and narrowly escaped a perilous fate at a steeple chase.

"How are you?" Asked our red horse.
"Oh, okay. Just thinking about my life lately. I think it's time for a change. I have much healing to do."

"What is it like where you come from?" asked the red horse with the female head.

"Oh, quite different from the peace you have here. I think you may get tired of the brutality and racing after a while. You wouldn't understand what I have suffered."

She fixed her yellow eyes on the red horse with an icy, unrelenting gaze. Then she flicked her tail and galloped off, carrying herself with an air of regal pride.

Our poor red horse stood alone. She had hurt herself. It bled and bled until it filled the sky until one could no longer see the sun. She drifted into slumber within the depths of the crimson night.

The Witch with a Tear in the Corner of Her Eye

Amongst us, there is a witch, or perhaps there are many. I know that I am one. I devise potions to make men fall in love with me. Most of the day, I sit and look out of my window.

"What's it all for?" I ask myself. "What do I want?"

"It's just this street and me. That's all there is." I feel a tear in the corner of my eye. "I mustn't cry," I think. I must move forward and never look back. I keep reminding myself, but we always do, don't we?

I remembered a young man who smiled at me today. Each time I pass him, I say, "Oh hello!" I try to act surprised, but he doesn't reply.

Time stands still now and again. One is left with an obvious sense of worldly exhaustion, as though when we halt and look outside our windows, we die for a moment and then take a pause before we gather inner strength once again.

He is the only one who can see that I am a witch with a tear in the corner of my eye.

CAROUSEL

There it stood, magnificent in pink and gold. No one knew quite why it was there, only that it had suddenly transpired. One afternoon, people had strolled quite indifferently past that desolate square. However, it was now impossible to ignore, for in its place stood a magnificent carousel. Its round base was intricately adorned with scrolls, mirrors, and gold, embellished with vividly coloured murals and unicorns.

The unicorns remained motionless, their slow breaths establishing a subtle connection with us. Then they went round and round, flying towards clouds of pink candy and the sound of laughter and music. During the nighttime, I would frequently visit them and watch as the lights and music gradually dispersed within the eerie fog. The music played softly; the kind you hear at old-fashioned fairgrounds. I could see the organ tubes moving up and down.

I would sit myself on my favourite pearly, silver, glittering unicorn, and around we would go! Sometimes we would ride through the sky and over the city. Those were my favourite moments. Years later, when I had given up hope in life, I walked through the forest, and there, amidst the trees, was an apparition: the carousel, lit up and adorned by the evening moon. It was silent and waiting for me.

ANGEL

Every so often, an angel flies down into my garden. She descends through the sky and over the tips of the grass and dandelions, gently gliding towards me. Her wings are a soft, feathered blue, and her skin seems lit up and almost strangely translucent. I can see the veins like blue ribbons, veiled behind thin silk. She seems lost but beautiful, an ethereal light and a face with tearful eyes.

It begins as an aura filled with hope and spiritual strength. She watches me, perhaps she is looking for a friend from long ago.

One day, I saw the angel asleep in my garden. She looked so peaceful, and I knew I had to step carefully through the grass so as not to disturb her. I hung the laundry on the washing line, and then I heard a strange, playful musical sound. When I turned around, the angel was humming softly. So, I walked over to her and asked how she was, and she turned toward me and gave me a look of despair.

"I've fallen by mistake," she said, "and cannot get back. Will you help me?"

It was a big decision for me. (I don't come across this situation often, you see, but the angel was real to me!)

That very same day, I leapt off a precipice, holding the angel's hand. I harboured the hope that this leap would transport me away from the earth towards flight. It was too late. I felt the pain, although it was quick. My body shattered into countless shards. I felt like a battered doll. I had helped someone find their way back. Now I was alone, lost, and ruined. My angel had forsaken me.

THE GLASS DOOR

There once lived a princess, so beautiful that all who set eyes upon her were said to fall under a very strange spell. Due to this, the princess lived alone in a huge palace in the center of the forest. People came to look for her, but they never returned, after catching a glimpse of her beauty. The princess had no idea what happened to them. One day she decided she

wanted to find out where they all disappeared to, as she had
remained uninformed for far too long. After all, she was so
lonely and had nothing to live for in this vast, wild forest by
herself.

And so it happened, as it usually did, that a prince came
walking through the woods. He had seen the golden spires of
her palace shimmering under the sun. As soon as the princess
saw him, she ran out among the trees towards him. But he
didn't seem to notice her. However, the princess secretly
followed him, and to her surprise, she saw the young man step
through a glass door in a clearing of bluebells and morning
dew.

The princess continued to walk quietly towards the glass door,
only to find that it disappeared immediately, much to her
disappointment.

For many weeks, the princess tried to follow her visitors, but
each time she did, they would walk through the glass door,
and then all would vanish. And so, it seemed there was only
one thing left to do. She would have to fall under the spell of
her image to solve this mystery.

One afternoon, she placed a large, beautiful mirror in the
forest, and in it was reflected the great wonder of nature itself,
so that all the trees, hills, birds, and rivers provided another
world to gaze into, more beautiful than anything.

And so, the princess began to walk into the woods to pick
flowers. On her return to the palace, she was suddenly caught
by surprise at her reflection in the mirror. Good, it had
worked! Before she had time to think, she fell into a deep
trance and began to walk through the trees toward the glass
door. If anyone had seen her, they would have been quite
mesmerised, for she looked so beautiful with her long black

hair shimmering with blue sparkles under the sun, and the trees casting an emerald hue over her pale skin.

Much to her wonder, the glass door suddenly opened, and she found herself walking inside a huge ballroom, so magnificent and wonderful. On the walls were carved gold faces and Cupids, and the ceiling was painted with cobalt blue, gold and pale pink goddesses transpiring through heavenly clouds.

There, inside the room, stood all the princes and princesses she had encountered, who because of setting eyes on her, had never returned to the palace. They were very welcoming and offered her food and wine. She began to dance for hours and even days. Everyone was wearing a Venetian mask that hid their identity. At one point she was kissed by a prince. It was all like an incredible dream, unreal, sensory, and surreal as she seemed to walk through one glass door after another.

But something was missing for the princess, something she couldn't quite define when being with these people. For a moment, she missed her beautiful palace in the woods. There was a strange and magical ballroom, but nothing was as strange and magical as her palace; absolutely nothing. Her palace was the most magnificent and mysterious of all palaces, and at that moment, she remembered the crystal bird that was perched on a tree in her lake. And each time you swam in that water, the bird would sing, and a fountain would flow from the flowers and the leaves.

For many years, people had tried to find the princess in the forest after hearing of her beauty. But now she was here, in this room, laughing and talking with everyone; her uniqueness had become quite normal, to say the least. After a while, the princess noticed that the prince did not instantly dance with her, and she wasn't the only person people wanted to be near or close to. Suddenly, the princess felt invisible, and strangely more invisible than when she was truly alone in the middle of the forest, inside her palace. This was not what she anticipated!

Feeling confused, she ran into another room where she cried, out of anxiety and exasperation. The next day, the princess decided she would return to her palace. But how could she do this and make everything the way it used to be? After all, nothing could be worse than living there alone as well as

45

being completely undesired. People would not want to desire her, not after they had known her. But in the end, there was no other solution as the princess had already become very bored with the prince and the guests.

After three days of searching, she finally discovered the glass door and calmly stepped through to the other side of the forest. She stretched her arms upwards toward the sky and thanked nature for all this beauty and she kissed the flowers in the grass, and she ran back to her palace.

As if by magic, everything changed back to normal, and once more the word got out that there was a beautiful princess who lived alone. But it was not the same, nor ever the same again. Instead of people walking through the glass door and never returning, they walked up to the princess, paid her compliments, and chatted with her about her mind and her thoughts.

The princess stood there, and for a moment, she felt quite sad. Why was she suddenly special? It wasn't right. Then she put a notice on the palace door saying, "Keep Out!" She found contentment in a solitary existence, choosing to dwell alone for all eternity, gathering wild mushrooms in the woods, and savouring the melodic trill of her crystal bird while taking moonlit swims in the enchanted lake.

THE QUEEN AND HER ANGRY SPIRIT

Once, in a distant land, a renowned Queen was celebrated for her wisdom. In her fifties, she remained attractive, and her youthful beauty remained the subject of hushed conversations. People sought her company, as she lived in solitude, save for occasional visits from her lover. She often sat at her spinning wheel, sharing stories of old with passers-by.

To view the Queen's angry spirit, flip the image.

One fateful night, as she sat by the fire, her thoughts drifted into the past, and for the first time in years, she found herself doubting. "Am I truly a kind person?" she wondered. "Or have I unwittingly earned disdain?" The desire to uncover her true friends consumed her.

On that very night, she confronted her long-time friend, who was visibly startled. However, the Queen demanded answers, persuading her to admit to an affair with the Queen's lover. Enraged, the Queen banished her from her presence. Subsequently, she awaited her beau's arrival, subjecting him to persistent interrogation until he confessed to not one but two affairs—one with her girlfriend and another woman.

The Queen's fury knew no bounds, leading her to expel him from her chambers. Alone and in tears, she pondered the swift shift from contentment to despair, perplexed by life's cruelty.

Suddenly, a knock at her door shattered her solitude. Opening it, she found an irate old woman. "I am your angry spirit," the crone declared, "and I have come to watch over you, lest you fall into despair." Pointing a crooked finger at the Queen, she continued, "Whenever wrath or doubt plagues you, call upon me thrice. I shall manifest and unleash my fury on your behalf." The Queen agreed, and when anger and doubt assailed her once more, she invoked her spirit thrice. The spirit appeared, embodying outrage and even inciting fear in the Queen.

The spirit then leapt at her and raged, leaving the Queen initially silent before bursting into laughter so intense that she had to sit down, her stomach aching from glee.
As fate would have it, the Queen encountered her former girlfriend in the forest. Rage welled up within her, and she grabbed the woman's hair. But then, she suddenly stopped and called her spirit thrice, which promptly appeared, pulling the woman's hair, spitting, and howling. The Queen stood contentedly, watching her spirit vent her anger. Yet, an unexpected thought crossed her mind—a memory of her girlfriend intervening to protect a young boy from bullies, which stirred guilt within the Queen and led her to order her spirit to cease.

Later that afternoon, the Queen spotted her beau riding through the forest. Fury again consumed her, and she accused him of infidelity. The prince, in fear of the Queen's wrath, became flustered. She screamed at him and summoned her spirit, who spat upon him and tore at his hair.

The Queen found amusement in the spectacle, revelling in her beau's torment. However, another unexpected thought struck her—a recollection of the prince rescuing a fox from a pack of hounds, gently placing it in his cloak until the hunters departed. The Queen commanded her spirit to stop and walked away, accompanied by a sense of loss.

Alone by the fire that night, the Queen contended with solitude and the realisation that she missed her companions. Betrayal still stung, and justifiably so. Nevertheless, she was a wise and venerable Queen. She approached the mirror and gazed at her reflection, acknowledging her fury, and recognizing that she had overstepped. But the most crucial question remained—had she been wrong?

ANNA'S WELL

I wrote 'Anna's Well' while travelling in Poland.
I wandered the countryside and enjoyed the handmade crafts
and sunflowers.

Once upon a time, in a quaint village nestled amidst emerald hills, lived a kind-hearted girl named Anna. She possessed the purest well in the village, so clear that it sparkled like a crystal in the morning light. Anna often gazed deep into its depths when feeling sad, yearning for the well to understand the whispers of her soul.

The village had fallen on hard times due to rumours of polluted water sources. No one knew the cause, and no official statement had been made, but the villagers weren't willing to take any risks. Anna's well, however, remained pristine and untainted, a source of comfort for her.

Every day at dawn, Anna collected water from her well and set off on her horse-drawn cart to deliver it to a remote village several miles away. The villagers there had come to rely on her clear, life-giving water, discovering their wells were contaminated.

Anna fulfilled her duty without fail, providing fresh, cool water to the villagers. Thanks, greeted her on each arrival, a routine that lasted for months. As the villagers grew more dependent on Anna's water deliveries, they stopped seeking official assistance in resolving the water pollution issue.

Initially worried about their contaminated wells, the villagers became complacent as Anna's deliveries continued. Her commitment saved them time and effort, and occasional treats from her added to their contentment. Over time, they took her deliveries for granted.

Months passed, and Anna's patience wore thin. She had her own life to live, caring for her ailing grandmother. When she inquired about progress in resolving the water issue, the villagers falsely assured her they were seeking official help.

With her kind nature, Anna continued her deliveries, increasingly sympathizing with the villagers' plight as they hid the truth from her.

A year later, the villagers had adjusted to their new routine. They no longer sought official help, and Anna struggled to balance caregiving with water deliveries. Forced to reduce her journey to just one, the villagers grew dissatisfied.

One villager's death, unrelated to the water issue, spurred the others to blame polluted water for the demise, deepening Anna's guilt. She increased her deliveries, hoping to help.

Frustrated, she confronted officials about their neglect, but they claimed ignorance. Villagers feigned gratitude for her concern.

Seeking help from the officials with a villager named Dereck, they were dismissed, causing Dereck to fabricate a story blaming Anna.

Realizing they couldn't continue the lie, the villagers planned to seize Anna's well and blame her.

Meanwhile, Anna's grandmother passed away, devastating her.

Dereck's lies led to Anna being punished by officials, leaving her helpless. Rescued by a passer-by, Anna requested to visit her well once more before peacefully passing away in her garden, thanking the well for its years of abundance.

Time passed, and the villagers, relying on Anna's well, discovered they could no longer access the water source. The well dried up, leading to drought and the villagers' demise due to their deceit.

Only Dereck remained, begging for help. The well responded to his tears, providing water under the condition of repairing contaminated wells and revealing the truth to officials. Completing the task, Dereck faced punishment, perishing in isolation.

The village recovered, learning a lesson about the consequences of deceit. Anna's well remained a symbol of purity and truth, teaching the importance of honesty in adversity.

THE STAG LADY

The Lady stood before her grand ornate mirror, gazing intently at her reflection. She scrutinized her body and the new dress she had acquired that very day, a vibrant tapestry of red flowers amidst intricate black lace. As her eyes travelled across her form, a peculiar sensation washed over her.

"How different I look these days," she mused, her thoughts deep and wistful. "Is it my hips or my breasts? Something about me has changed." Unbeknownst to her, her reflection began to waver, the contours of her face and body shifting like an elusive dream.

Gradually, she became aware of the transformation, though not in the way one might expect.

The once-familiar features of her visage underwent a metamorphosis. Her head sprouted long, textured horns that gracefully curved from her skull. As the bony protrusions extended, there was an odd sense of rightness, as if these magnificent antlers had always belonged there.

The bone structure of her face shifted, embracing the essence of a majestic stag, a creature of the woods. She blinked; the world was seen through the eyes of a graceful forest Queen.

"Yes, I certainly haven't lost my looks," she thought, the awareness of her new form settling in as naturally as the change itself. "It's my breasts that have changed." And so, she convinced herself, her mind finding comfort in small untruths.

Yet, as her eyes darted downward, they fell upon her unchanged, untouched breasts, steadfast in their form. Her self-deception was a mere illusion, a consequence of the enchantment that had befallen her. The Lady, now graced with the head of a stag, continued to admire her new reflection, a fusion of woman and woodland creature, her perception veiled in the curious and wondrous realm of the magical dawn.

THE KISS

One afternoon, I strolled through Santa Fe, appreciating the faded pastel hues and sleek adobe structures. It was a joyful day in my life. Everything was shifting, and I was oblivious to the transition out of my mid-twenties. The sun blazed down, causing the light to dance playfully over turquoise and pink facades. Everywhere I gazed, I felt excitement at each turn, through every window, mirroring the sun, as if people were watching over me, summoning me from other realms.

I decided to sit down and enjoy a coffee, pondering my next set of plans. Where should I go? What should I do? Should I go to Key West and meet Valerie? At times, it seemed as though I attracted peculiar incidents into my life.

Across from me, a man caught my eye as he savoured his cigarette. How remarkably handsome he was, with his dusky complexion, cream sombrero and Mexican charm; he possessed a captivating beauty. I admired his coarse ebony hair and his obsidian eyes, which reflected both passion and battles, reminiscent of Zapata and rebellion.

Clad in a Seventies rendition of The Good, The Bad, and the Ugly, he stood with an air of nobility, resembling an Aztec King in stature.

Suddenly, as if locked in telepathy, he approached me, took my hand, and then we shared an intimate kiss. He led me to a bar where hummingbirds flitted amidst the dahlias. We savoured tequila and exchanged affectionate kisses in the soft illuminated corner of those corridors, where lovers were meant to embrace and laugh, where time appeared to stand still, leaving only the two of us in motion while all others seemed frozen in time. They watched us because we evoked memories of their youth and freedom, reminding them of their dreams, their past, and perhaps their future.

And so, there we were on that hazy afternoon. We engaged in conversation and meandered through the square, which lay deserted except for the gentle chiming of bells in the wind. Eventually, we bid each other farewell, and I never set eyes on him again.

MEXICO

The scorching sun, the gilded desert—I see turquoise mosaic jewellery adorning a woman's delicate wrist. This image is redolent of a Mayan Princess, the calm strength of her face against the warm adobe wall beckoning me toward an enchanted kingdom.

The boy escorts me to his grandfather's garden, an image reminiscent of a naive painting with pastel hues. He points to the sacred wall of white-painted stone and gentle earth, which cradles a substantial gem casket with the Virgin gazing out at me, encircled by yellow, red, and pink synthetic roses. She weeps for the world, and no amount of rational thought can elucidate the tears on her face.

A cobalt-painted serpent winds along the sinuous branch and glides over the glass, evoking Cleopatra with the asp or Snow White encased in her glass coffin, destined to receive the kiss before she chokes on a morsel of a poisoned apple. Each tiny crevice in the wall harbours devoted objects: a candle, a fractured mirror, or a faded picture.

All these things fill me with recollections, soothing my mind, preventing me from gradually fading and becoming a hallucination, like a corroded animal skeleton in the Nevada desert.

One anticipates Guadeloupe to glide across the horizon, dusting roses beneath her feet, allowing the linings of our coats to be imprinted with the same crimson roses that have now disappeared from the ground. All this, so that I may rush to a church and exclaim, "Look who I have seen!"

The young girl peddles fresh papaya, coated in fiery chili pepper. It takes a while for my taste buds to adjust. She awaits my passage, hoping that I will purchase the fruit, as I walk across the bridge from El Paso. The man gazes at me from beneath his broad, white-brimmed hat. His eyes are tormented and dusky, scrutinizing me until he has amassed all the information he requires.

I continue to meander as if stepping through a painting, only to find myself ensconced within that composition, encircled by the argent, white trees, the elderly woman gazing at the train, the children imploring for money, and a stray dog. The memory calls to me, drawing me in like a hypnotic spell cast by the desert and the vivid turquoise depths of my fate.

THE MUSIC ROOM

Smoke ascends into the air, creating circular drawings, the kind you dream about while you sit there and observe their faces. The smoke swirls around the room gracefully, like a group of spirits who cannot leave until they have analyzed and caressed our faces and cold hands, warming them silently. It curls in and out of our fingers and around our heads, searching for our souls and crying out to us in our subconscious, "We're here if you need us."

Someone opens a window, and the smoky apparitions flow outside, they hold on to each other as they glide towards their world.

The banjo harmonizes with the accordion, and one girl drums near her face as if she were a Greek statue brought to life, positioned in a music alcove. The man with the guitar is softened by the muted glow. His sweater, the colour of emeralds commands attention like a verdant mossy slope, arranged for someone to recline upon, to gently caress and comfort him.

The girl with the accordion improvises. It has become her. All her vitality courses through her physique and into the supple and sensual body of that instrument, so that from afar, when she is motionless, one can perceive the accordion germinating from her as if she were coming forth from a cocoon, gradually and quietly, imperceptible to those around her.

Like some peculiar insect, she will continue to play her music while she gradually blossoms. Eventually, she can perch on the softness of the mossy slope, while she metamorphoses.

Once this takes place, she becomes the clear sound, the fresh tune, the new achievement of the celestial spirit, within the music room. The girl with the drum will then softly beat from her musical pergola and everyone will continue to play their instruments, lost in their musings, oblivious to the outside world.

THE TREE

The neighbours are always complaining about the tree outside my window. All day the tree murmurs with her splendid green leaves delicately dancing in the breeze. She is very vain and proud of her leaves like some of us are about our hair.

"Hurry, hurry," the tree murmurs, "time is running out if you want to get there."

"Get there?" I ask. "Where do I want to go?"

"Ah," she murmurs again and then she laughs with the melodious sound of tinkling bells and her splendid green hair flows in the wind.

The tree is my friend. She understands my troubles. When I tell her I've been arguing with my husband, she just laughs and tells me, "This too will pass, this too will pass."

One day, I came home from work. The neighbour was in my garden. He was holding an axe. He was smiling at his hard day's work.

"What are you doing!" I asked.

"Getting rid of this tree," he replied because it blocks out the light."

"NO!" I cried, but he wouldn't listen.

I was heartbroken when I saw my friend lying there in pieces all over the brown earth, her limbs here and everywhere. I bent down and kissed her.

"Goodbye, my beloved friend."

The man joked around. He thought I was mad talking to a tree.

That evening I heard a scream. People from the house ran downstairs. The neighbour was crying frantically.

"What has happened?" cried the tenants.

"My husband!" she screamed.

Her husband lay lifeless beneath the tree, appearing serene, almost as if he had melded into the tree's embrace, as though the great tree had woven its roots around him, merging him into its primaeval form.

THE LANDLORD

My landlord used to knock on my door. I always wondered, "Is it my money this time, or my company?" He didn't say much; he would just gaze at my paintings. I didn't know what he was doing in my room, but somehow, I think he liked it there.

Then the time came to say goodbye. After all, I had my adventure to continue.

"Goodbye," he said on the stairs.

"I'll be in touch," I replied.

"No, you won't," he answered.

He was right. I never did because it's too late. I should have met him back in the 1950s. It's sadly all too late.

Sometimes I dream about him. He's waving to me in another dimension while dancing to Elvis.

MOLE

The pavement is so cold; it will crush me one day between its icy grey slates. Beneath the earth, I will tell the insects a story and teach them how to get rid of those awful mole traps. A poor mole with his harmless mound and secret tunnel. How many will have their paws covered in blood today?

The grey slates will cover my grave, and people will walk over me, more worried about their unscratched shoes, little knowing I am having a secret conversation with the insects. I'll be teaching them how to get rid of those mole traps so that the moles can scuffle freely in and out of winding hills and desolate gardens, brightening up the emerald, green grass with an air of audacity, where the brown earth makes small slopes all in a row. Some here and there and everywhere. Whatever happens, the mole must continue his journey!

EVEN THOUGH

In the silence, the leaves rustled like curious whispers, questioning, "What lies on your itinerary today, Alice?" Yet, amidst the warmth of the sun's embrace on my winter coat, a melancholic mood smothers me.

Even as I drift into visions of a beautiful island, far from the veneer of artificial smiles and repetitive dialogues, and envision myself beneath a canopy of filtering sunlight, darkness lingers, shrouding everything in the gloom. And the reason eludes me.

This morn, snow cascaded gently onto the ground, akin to an array of delicate feathers descending upon the town. It felt as though aeons had passed since I found myself ensconced within the blossom of life, where fairy tales wove their narratives and spun intricate tales. I ponder, where might Bobby Shafto be? Does he still roam the seas? I had intended to gift him a silver pair of buckles, but he had departed for the sea without a farewell. He looked so sad, and we never had the chance to say farewell.

THE SWAN

Sitting beside the river, I noticed the silent green pastures surrounding the moist, overgrown area of reeds and water. I would often just lie back and listen to the breeze. There wasn't a soul around except for the white swan, which often glided to and towards me, and then away again, around the curve of the lake until he had disappeared.

For many years, I had come to this spot. Once I had called the swan, and he appeared in the distance. It was almost as though it knew me. One afternoon I saw the swan gliding across the lake, and he was wearing a golden crown. Silly me for not noticing before.

Many days, I would wander down to the river and see him with his golden crown, radiant in the sun. And then one day he spoke to me.

"You weren't supposed to know about this," he shouted, and he looked very angry. I was scared when I heard him talk and shuddered inside. I was about to make excuses when I thought, how ridiculous! And replied, "Well, you can't expect to keep a secret like that forever!"

He looked shocked and swam towards me.
"Why are you a man with a swan's head?" I asked.
"Because I never awoke from my dream," he replied.
Astonished, I asked him what it was he dreamt.

"Well," he said, "I was in love with a beautiful woman. But just as I was about to wake up, she turned me into a swan. It shocked me so much that I was caught in between my dream and reality, and so far, have never made it back."

"Oh," I replied, rather listlessly, hoping that I wasn't dreaming all this myself.

Afterwards, we went to sleep, and I began to dream that I too was turning into a bird. In my dream, I also became pregnant. When I awoke, the swan had disappeared.

But a while later, I gave birth. I never met the swan man again. Eventually, I returned my little cygnet to that same lake where I had first met his father.

"He needs you," I said, and I walked the lane and fields back home.

WALKING IN THE SKY

She often slept in the clouds, watching the changing seasons. First, it was snowflakes, then flower petals, and finally, autumn leaves. It was a joy to lie on a bright, sunlit cloud, breathing in the fresh, warm air and looking down at the icy mountaintops.

Two people lay in a meadow with their backpacks ready for a challenging climb. They would pause to drink dandelion and burdock. The sun danced on the rocky path, their legs ached, and one panted heavily. But what mattered most was the realisation that this moment, with no one else around but a friend, was unmatched in its solitude.

I yearn to escape, sail the sea, explore vast forests, and sleep among the cool, crisp leaves with insects whispering in my ear. The greatest pleasure would be to not know what the next day holds and to let everyone experience the feeling of walking in the sky.

When Mother was a young girl, she used to glide across the playground with ease. It was simple – just a leap and a short run, and then she was in the air. "I wish that could happen to me," I said.
"It will," she assured.

During her flight, high in the clouds like a fairy queen, she lost her crown one morning, and it fell with a loud crash, splitting in two. One piece fell into the ocean, sinking until it reached a bed of silvery sand. The other half landed in a snowy field and was quickly covered by leaves bedecked with dew.

THE STREAM

One solitary tree in the distance, a few skipping lambs, and my feet submerged in the stream with pebbles and stones beneath me. I stand and listen to the whispering of the water, that peculiar, indescribable sound; a language that is challenging to articulate, a kind of rushing, gentle murmur. I hear the birds and watch a raven dart here and there, exploring the dewy field.

The stream seemed to be speaking to me. Was it a brushing, shushing sound, or was it more like bubbling, akin to a sea wave? I can't quite envision it. All I recall is that it immersed itself in my thoughts. The water appeared so green and translucent, like a green ribbon. It flowed through my dreams until it succumbed to the heavy pattering of the rain.

In my dream, there was a woman with emerald hair and green eyes. When she spoke, her voice was as gentle and benevolent as nature itself, her skin as smooth as silk. She concealed her thoughts behind the soft pearly clouds. She seemed delicate and sad. But her soul was as unyielding as that obsidian mountain.

FIREFLY

I feel like fire today, as angry as a wildfire, cheated and disappointed with life. This morning, I wandered through an arch of emerald leaves dappling the sky like a mosaic of green illuminated glass. This provided comfort after a morning filled with regret and anger. Why do I feel empty today? It's because my efforts have not been rewarded. All those days of work, all those sacrifices, and still, they seem futile.

Bite and fight
Bite and fight
Say the creatures of the night!

A strange rustling noise, an emptiness running through me, whispering, "No hope." Only yesterday, I was aglow with delight. Even the river was on my side. This morning it was serene and melancholic and yesterday, it was shimmering brightly like a precious stone in the golden sun.

Bite and fight
Bite and fight
Say the creatures of the night!

KNIGHTS OF THE SWORD

The ice enhanced their worn faces. Brutality had swept away fear, and now all that remained was a sword to slice through flesh. It would produce one ecstatic scream because the weight of time carries so much pain and so much joy.

The horses scuffed the ice as flowing capes billowed in the ancient fields, surrounded by bloodshed that had witnessed so much before and would witness much more to come.

The ice absorbed the thick blood until it congealed, like a wound, a crimson cross on an abstract white canvas. And all that echoed were the melodies of sparrows in the age-old woodland amidst Gothic ambiences.

THE WIFE OF BRIGHTON

I think I'll die today. Yes, it's time to die. I've had some fun, have said my bit and now it's time to depart. Fare-thee-well old world. You've done me kind and done me rotten, but I don't care because today I'm going to die.
Fresh white sheets and red roses in a vase, the window open. I'll wear a white lace nightgown, but first I'll make myself clean. Once I've combed my hair I'll put on my beloved jewellery and perfume, put some fresh flowers in a vase and then I'll just lie there and wait to die.
Death, here I come!

RED POLISH

She observes my red nails digging into my thigh. "Red nails and red lips don't belong here," I can feel them thinking. They scrutinize my face with my shiny red lips and black mascara. I appear artificial. However, these red nails hail from a world of Hispanic kisses and desert dreams. My lips act as a shield before I utter a word.

My red nails play with the pendant around my neck. Yet, their gaze remains fixed on my red nails. What are they contemplating? Maybe they consider me one of those women from the magazines.

"Get rid of her!" they shout and before I know it, they have locked me in a dark cage. I can see them staring at me with their vile expressions of disdain.

"Come on, ladies," I say, "We're all in the same boat, aren't we? All part of the same team and such."

The next time, I refrain from wearing red nail polish. It's too contentious, sparking too much commotion and animosity. Sometimes people will detest you.

"Red is to shock, to alert; it is also sexual," a woman whispers in my ear.

"But it's only red polish," I reply. "Is that so bad?"

"Yes, it is," she replies. "If you want to be one of *us*, then never again, never again, never!"

JIGSAW

He concentrates on the jigsaw, slowly and carefully fitting each little piece next to the right one. First, the sky; then the mountains; then the rocks; and finally, the earth. So carefully, so thoughtfully, he ensures that each section blends with the other.

It takes all my effort to catch his eye, but he continues with the jigsaw. If only he could concentrate on me in that way. He could piece together each part of my mind, learn to understand my desires and grasp the structure and strength of my desires. Finally, he could understand my spirit. How happy we would be.

When he had pieced me all back together again, he could leave me intact and admire me every so often, just like the jigsaw. Eventually and inevitably, he would come and mess me up all over again.

TIME TO LAUGH

"Chin up, girl," how I hate that phrase. A pat on the back, life's okay, really, and all that nonsense. I paint my face pale, not silver, because I want to look like a vampire.

Oh yes, remember those times we laughed? We laughed so much we hurt our insides. There was this complete lack of self-consciousness on our part. We just weren't there; we were simply laughing so much. I think we would have been content even if our guts had fallen out.

"Oh, you funny face, you funny person. Isn't it all so wonderful? Isn't it?"

There is silence.

"Yes," she replies, "but we're not real."

She places her hand on my shoulder. It's like a whisper, but I feel it all the same. This is what life's about, and we face each other silently. "Yes, this is what it's all about." Only, we can't keep it up, and instead, we just roll about laughing.

GREEN CHAIR

The green chair sits invitingly in front of me, with a complimentary Turkish red carpet beneath it. It seems to exert a certain authoritative influence over me. If it were human, it would be "bohemian", a woman who aspires to emulate Isadora Duncan.

Once, its green velvet cover used to welcome me like a witch's cauldron, mysterious and present. But, it appears too shiny, today, like seaweed. "Oh, darkness," it utters, "you dwell in darkness because you feel no hope. You're teetering on a fragile precipice that could break at any moment."

At times, I imagine the chair dwelling beneath the water. It's home to a mermaid who has seen her share of days and now reclines there, quietly assessing all the sea creatures, her silver tail rippling through the underworld of waves, isolated from the concerns of the world.

Then, one day, the chair transforms into a massive cave on an island, consumed and concealed by time. Sometimes, I feel like I have been fractured into pieces. I am directionless, somewhere out there, in the ocean, a bottle with a message inside bobbing along, under the moonlight, lost and abandoned, a story that destiny has chosen to conceal, forever like a terrestrial phantom.

THE MERMAID'S TAIL

In this story, a mermaid gracefully swam through ancient caverns, basking in the sunlight's gentle touch as it perforated the water, illuminating the oceanic fauna below.
.

The mermaid enjoyed rising to the surface and exploring the world above the sea. One day, she persuaded a sea witch to help her walk on land. The sea witch granted her request but then banished her with a stern warning.

Suddenly, the mermaid found herself encased inside a beautiful seashell on the beach, large enough for a person to take shelter in.

She had dreamt of stumbling upon enchanting melodies as if lifted from the pages of an age-old poem or a mystical fairy tale. Instead, she heard a rhythmic, clattering sound, much like castanets from a Spanish dance. Briefly, she envisioned being enveloped by flamenco dancers, a surreal escape from the pressures in her life.

She yearned for a love imbued with passion, desiring the company of the most handsome man in the realm. Previously, she had engaged in playful flirtations with different mermen, exploring the choices at her disposal.

She listened to the clacking sound growing louder as she lay inside her seashell on the sandy shore. There in the distance was a cowboy riding a black horse, resembling a character from a movie. It felt as if he could shatter her seashell and steal her breath in an instant.

With determination, she made up her mind that if death were to come, she would face it on her feet. Emerging from her seashell, she lifted her arms high, reminiscent of the bold women from fifties car races. Defiantly, she dared the cowboy, yelling, "Come and take me on! I'm not scared of you!"

The cacophony of clattering reached a fever pitch, resonating through the air's ethereal tapestry. Confronted by the mermaid, he observed the absence of her tail. In a desolate tone mirroring the arid expanse, he queried, "Where's your tail?"

"I don't have one," she responded.

The cowboy sank his teeth into her feet, eliciting a scream that triggered the miraculous regeneration of her tail. Yet, he callously severed it again, savouring the consumption over a fire nestled in the mountains of Idaho.

Rumours persist beneath the waters that the mermaid's tail was not devoured by a cowboy in Idaho but continues to sway among the waves. Some claim she met her demise due to an excess of love and that she found her match in the world above.

GHOST

Sometimes the waves almost reach her feet. Back and forth, she jumps, playing with the curling white spirals on the sand, laughing, and throwing pebbles; she always escapes the water. One afternoon, she was out sailing, but the boat sank, and she spiralled deep into the sea. No one found her again. Her father

often returns to the beach to talk with her spirit. The little boat
is still washed up and in pieces on the shore.
Sometimes he thinks he sees her standing there amidst the
waves. He runs toward her, but she slips back into the sea. He
never catches her. She always escapes.

REFLECTIONS

Cat women stand near the lake. They stand in a long line
beneath the shady trees. The reflections from the moon cast
rippling lights over their cat faces, and their eyes glint and
flicker. Their tails curl around their bodies like feather boas,
and their claws move in and out of their hands like
mechanical things.

"Let's go for a drive," said Rita, the leader cat lady. She and
her friends jumped in the car and drove through the moonlit
lanes up to the moors where the mist hovered over the
primeval walls like something out of a Gothic fairy tale.

Eventually, they reached a pub called The Devil's Elbow. As
they walked inside, everyone glanced strangely at them. The
cat women looked at them, blinked, and curled their tails
around each other. Standing regal in red velvet capes, their
yellow almond eyes glistened in the dark, smoky room.

"We are here to sing to you," the cat women said.
But one man in the room became angry. He stood up and hit
Rita over the head, causing her to fall and cut her furry cheek.

"Meow!" howled the cat women. The people looked frightened, and the man regretted what he had done and walked slowly backwards and away from them.

It was too late. The cat women eventually stood back, content with their claws covered in blood. A haunting silence enveloped the room, broken only by the distant melody of the jukebox playing Country and Western music in the background.

Outside The 'Elbow', they saw their reflections of beautiful cat women, standing amidst trees and lakes, merged with the clouds, lit up by the moon. They saw a reflection of Rita turning into a bird after she had eaten the bird itself. They saw another reflection of Rita turning into a fish after she had eaten the fish, and she swam and flew while the other cat women tried to catch her reflection because they were tempted to eat her.

But when Rita saw them scratching at her reflection, she cried loudly and told them to stop! The cat women turned to her with their large curious yellow eyes.
"All reflections are real," said Rita. "They are no less real than we. What exists is alive, and by eating my reflection, you are eating me!"

"Meow?" replied the cat woman. And they wandered into the forest, concerned and contemplating Rita's words. After a while, they became increasingly hungry, and Rita's reflection of the bird and the fish followed them and tempted them more each day. But they resisted and went to sleep as beautifully as possible on the cushioned forest terrain.

That night, all their reflections visited them. The reflections included fish, birds, mice, insects, and even men. All the things they enjoyed eating most.

Rita's friends heard the rustling in the grass of all those strange creatures, and then they woke up and pounced on every creature, seized hold of them, and devoured them with much pleasure.

The following day, there were no reflections of the cat women in the lake. Very soon they realised they must have eaten them. So sad were they, not to admire their beautiful selves, those almond yellow eyes and red boas and sharp claws like mechanical things. So sad were they that they could no longer see their beauty, until one day they could cope no more, and they turned to Rita and said, "It was *you* who said that your reflection was real! *You* said we could go hungry until we could go hungry no more! *You* said your reflection was as real as *you*!"

Rita's eyes enlarged and twinkled as they said this.
"We want our reflections back!" said the cat women, and they pounced and began devouring her on the spot.

Poor Rita lay there, dead, and the cat women embalmed her and placed her underneath the water so that when they looked on the surface, they would, at last, have a reflection, no less real than the one they had eaten. The fish swam around Rita and slowly nibbled away her red cloak. The insects laid their eggs in her fur, and the mice took their revenge while the birds pecked out her eyes until there was no longer a reflection left for the other cat women.

That night, they sat and wept. The tears flowed for Rita, oh beautiful Rita. They wept for their reflections, and as they rose, their wails echoed to the moon. Across the land, a haunting 'meow' resonated. They pleaded with the birds to grant them reflections and begged the mice and fish. "Be our reflections!" they cried. Yet, the creatures remained indifferent. In the end, all the cat women perished, as life seemed devoid of meaning without their reflections or beauty.

One day, a group of sailors discovered their claws and fashioned necklaces out of them, for their mistresses in distant lands. When night fell and the men slept, the claws emitted an eerie glow under the moon, moving in and out like mechanical apparitions.

THE WITCH

She resides at the pinnacle of an old beech tree. The sun illuminates the amber leaves, and people can hear her laughing at night and singing in the morning. Her laugh is one of those that burst out from the lungs, as though she is taunting you, and her singing echoes like a talented girl who composes songs for herself. No one has ever seen her; just a pale, slim arm, reclining down through the branches. The hand of this arm sprinkles golden dust on the foreheads of people and animals. They arrive with gilded and silver goblets, which they tie to the branches with vines. Some stand below and gaze upwards. The people eat the dust-like confections. What they always thought was candy was a serum to cure jealousy and sometimes addiction. But mainly, it is dust to make them see the beauty in everything.

In this surreal realm, azure waters cascade down steep hills, giving birth to butterflies crafted from miniature beings. These tiny figures whisper enchanting words into the ear of a witch, draping their lavender wings around her shoulders to protect her. The sun transforms everything into a copper glow, while snow delicately coats the winding pathways. Amidst this whimsical landscape, everyone frolics in the snow, while elders bask in the sun. Horned beasts ferry people back and forth, and winged creatures carry the people across the valleys through rainbows, sunshine, and storms.

From the beech tree, the witch's pale arm dangles, as people depart with their goblets filled with golden dust. Husbands and wives transform their jealousy into happiness, and the children's eyes gaze with wonder. But there is one man who has fallen in love with the witch. He has seen nothing but her pale arm and delicate hand, suspended from an abyss of obsidian branches and golden leaves.
He often reaches upward to see if he can sense her, but nothing is there except the dark tree and her voice. "Go home and waste no time with me," she says, "for I will only bring you sorrow. You cannot love a witch like me."

But the man does not listen and imagines her as the beauty of his dreams. This continues for many weeks until the witch has no choice but to come down from her tree and reveal who she is. When this happens, even the man is struck with wonder at the beauty he beholds. The witch stands there in a golden haze, and her pale skin is iridescent amidst her pale robe, and her auburn hair, like autumn leaves, settles like a fire over her pale shoulders.

Each day, the man visits his witch and admires her beauty, but she soon tires of this and tells him that his constant appearance makes her weary. To remedy this, she concocts a solution – she pours silver dust into his goblet. Now, whenever he wishes to see her, he can release the dust into the air, summoning her illusion. The witch believes this will satisfy him, but alas, it fails.

After a while, he grew weary of the enchanted dust and yearned for her in the flesh. So, the witch transformed herself into a repugnant old hag. She reveals herself to the man until he no longer longs for her, leaving him to weep inconsolably, forever mourning the loss of his once beautiful lady of the tree.

BENEATH THE EARTH

Beneath the Earth's surface, another world exists. Two lovers, drawn there by chance, frequently find themselves within its vibrant depths. With a fearless disposition, they guide the giant insects towards the waterfall for their daily drink, and the others to the bank, adorned with twigs and moss. Dragonflies flutter through the air, and peculiar, melodic echoes resonate in the underground world. The grass rustles softly as if welcoming the passage of invisible feet. In the distance, a flock of black crows creates intricate patterns against the backdrop of a golden field with their graceful wingbeats.

This is the time of year when winged horses take flight below the Earth's surface. We are joyful as we mount the silky, white, velvet-backed steeds. The horses gallop through, the Earth, weaving through the labyrinthine roots of trees like mysterious spectres. Their white coats and wings are illuminated as if they were painted on the base of a breathtaking Grecian urn.

The mystic lady knows that one day she will encounter someone who can journey beneath the ground on a winged horse. There, they will share endless laughter throughout the day and night, until their laughter melds into a harmonious, inexplicable voice that beckons, "Fly away with me."

Lovers will slumber eternally beneath the watchful gaze of the stars and the moon. They rest perpetually, cradled by the interplay of shadows in the night.

A BURIAL

The long pathway meandered into the distance, vanishing among a cluster of trees. A lady stood there, wearing a red velvet cape. As I passed by, she smiled with her red velvet lips, and I continued to ascend until I reached a small depression in the ground. I walked around its circumference for a while. It started to rain, and the depression began to fill, bearing the semblance of a surreal aquatic void in the ground.

Emerging from the obscure depths, a visage materialized before me, seemingly a reflection at first. But the countenance articulated a warning: "Do not venture further down this course.

I initially thought this was absurd since I walked this path every day. "Do not go! " The visage persisted. Then she faded, leaving me alone to decide.

There were miles ahead of me, and I couldn't discern anything unusual. The trees adorned their customary tranquillity in the warm sun, and the fields were fresh and serene. So, I continued. However, after half an hour of wandering, I noticed something ahead on the path, something peculiar and dark, easily mistaken for a fluttering black plastic bag. As I drew nearer, the unfamiliar shape transformed into an injured cat with its paw caught in a trap. Angrily, yet with notable weakness, it writhed in pain.

Slowly and gently, I knelt and released the jaws of the trap, setting the cat free. Painfully, it limped onto the path and gazed up at me, its eyes so green and penetrating that I felt uneasy. "Go on!" I urged. "Off you go!" Only it didn't depart. Instead, it grew until it reached the size of a puma. Terrified, I realised I had no choice but to follow my feline friend.

She led me through a hedge, and the scent was sweet, reminiscent of roses and honey. As we ventured further, I stumbled upon a pond, and once again, the visage appeared in the reflection, cautioning me not to proceed. I paused for a moment. The cat gazed at me but did not attempt to stop me. To test it, I walked away, and it didn't follow. I remained free and could leave whenever I wished. So, I chose to continue following the cat. When I turned around, it patiently awaited me, and we resumed our journey. I couldn't help but wonder where we were heading.

The brambles and thorns began to graze my arms, and it was then that we reached our destination. The cat stood still and then lay down sadly in the grass. I ventured a bit further and spotted a deep pit, where at the bottom lay a deceased puma impaled on massive stakes. I couldn't believe it—a trap for a wild animal in this gentle forest? Panic washed over me, suddenly. "Why had the cat led me here? What could I possibly do?" I pondered. I recalled the warning from the face in the pond and felt a sense of impending danger. Perhaps, the cat wants revenge, to see me perish in place of its mate, I surmised. As I looked up, the cat's green eyes bore into my thoughts, and my heart pounded loudly.

After a while, I realised this was not a sight for the cat to see. I imagined myself in her position. I would want someone to help my dead lover, to pull out the stakes and bury that person properly. So, I climbed inside the pit, and after pushing away vines and twigs, I managed to haul the puma from the pit while my friend pulled the cord from above with her teeth. My hands were covered in blood. The poor animal had suffered terrible butchery. The stakes glared up at me from below with abhorrence. My companion tenderly cleaned her mate, and we carried him to a meadow where I excavated a hole, adorning it with flowers.

There, we buried the puma. However, just as I was about to cover it with earth, the cat also jumped in, and I realized what was required of me. I felt sad and needed time to think about this. The cat seemed to plead with me until eventually, I gave in and buried them both together in the earth. On top of the mound, I placed flowers and leaves. I thought I could hear crying from below, and within myself, I felt as if I were crying, imagining those beautiful cats embraced in love in death. I walked away, feeling empty. For a moment, I envied the cat. Why couldn't I love like that?

As I walked away, the visage in the pond said, "I told you not to go, I told you so."

THE DINNER

We sat opposite each other at the table. Silence hung in the air as we glanced at the sepia photographs on the walls. Accents were subtly exaggerated, and we heard the tinkling and chiming of crockery. I caught a glimpse of a woman serving coffee. "It's rather hot, like a mad hatter's tea party, isn't it?" she announced.

Crackers were pulled, and a thin, transparent fortune-telling red fish popped out, which I placed in the palms of those curious about their fortunes. How could I tell the quiet one that she was jealous? The other lady was passionate and in love.

It's strange to observe people's faces. The betrothed meddles silently with the fish. The boss laughs when it lands in her hand. "What does it mean?" she asks. She giggles and is thinking about her lover, and I must avoid the subject of my lover, so I explain its meaning.

My neighbour talks of colours and spiced dishes never eaten by ourselves. She falls into the dreams of her lover, who journeys from shores untraveled by our feet. She talks of his vibrant home, and you can see she wants to kiss him, but he's not there. "Where is he?" she wonders, "where is he?"

My boss peers down the length of the table, her eyes like a demon. Our souls do not meet. Instead, we always collide clumsily.

When there is silence at our end, there is laughter at the other, and when there is laughter with us, there is silence with them. We formed two halves, two separate worlds. The tablecloth is ashen, like our faces. We laugh and yet we cry. The fruit lies on my plate as though someone had cut out our insides and placed them before me. All the symbols of fruit passed through my mind. As I ate the apple, I thought of my temptations. As I ate the guava and melon, I thought of Frida Kahlo's revolutionary paintings. As I drank my wine, I looked along the table and felt as if I was a disciple casting out my sins. But Judas was there and not Jesus. We talked, we ate, we let time fade, and then continued with our work.

But I still remember the boss with her fish as it turned over in her hand. "Did she lie?" she thought. "Yes, I did," I whispered back to her in my mind. We glanced briefly at one another. I walked away in silence, and I felt I had seen enough. Such sad faces I will never forget.

A DEMON

Some sabotaged trees that had once stood tall and swaying now stood forlornly on a sunlit day. Vandals had visited during the night. They had broken the branches and stamped the flowers, and what was once a heavenly corridor of lush leaves was now desolate and bland.

From a tree emerged a demon. Ancient and weary, with a white beard cascading to the ground, his skin shrivelled and weathered, and his attire tattered. One fateful day, the demon discovered a vandal carving into his tree, his abode celebrated for its three-century-old bark. And there was the vandal, chopping away at it! In response, the demon leapt out, startling the intruder, declaring, "I have caught you! You shall face consequences unless you undertake two tasks for me.

The vandal, mockingly standing there, dared not risk the demon's punishment. Reluctantly, he agreed to carry out two tasks.

The first task was to destroy the small tree in the corner of the field. The vandal, confused, sadistically took out his knife to carve into the young tree's rich bark. As he did this, the knife slid, cutting his finger. In pain, he kicked the tree, only to injure himself further. In total agony, he lay on the ground, but he was inspired to destroy the tree. Climbing into its branches, he began to cut them one by one, losing his balance and falling to the ground, lucky not to have broken his leg.

The demon, seeing this, laughed, then hobbled over, shouting, "You have failed! You now have only one task left, and if you fail, I shall give you your just punishment."

The demon's second task was to burn the tree. Again, the vandal was confused. Determined to win, he hid inside the tree to see what the demon would do. When the demon returned, he laughed heartily. "Come out! You have not completed your task."

Refusing to come out, the vandal challenged the demon. "If you want me to burn this tree, I refuse, and therefore I have won. I am protected. If this tree wishes to hurt me, it will also be hurt."

"Come out, you fool!" shouted the demon. "You must burn the tree. You do not know how lucky you will be."

"No!" shouted the vandal. "I am staying here because I know I am safe as long as you want this tree to stay alive. That, I believe, is what you want, and therefore I have won."

"Believe as you will," replied the demon. "My reason is not the same as yours, and if you do not burn the tree, I shall claim my due from you."

The vandal remained inside the tree but suddenly saw the demon in the distance lighting a fire, his face now angry. "You have refused," the demon shouted, "and because of this, you will be severely punished if you don't answer two questions truthfully."

The vandal agreed, thinking it was easy. "First question," said the demon. "Why are you destroying my home, and secondly, why do you not burn the tree?"

"I shall answer you," said the vandal, "and then I will ask you a question."

"Go ahead and answer," laughed the demon.

The vandal, looking around him, said, "The reason I destroy your home is because I enjoy it and the reason I will not burn the tree is because I do not trust you."

The demon rolled around, laughing. "Now you wish to ask me a question, don't you?"

This was the vandal's final chance, and he crawled closer inside the tree for protection. "My question is why do you want me to burn the tree?"

The demon hobbled over to the fire, picked up a dry branch, and lit it with a flame. The vandal stared in horror but dared not emerge from the tree until he had his answer. Before he could even think of reasons for the demon's actions, the demon hurled the lit branch toward him, and suddenly the tree burst into flames.

In the distance, the vandal's desperate cries for help could be heard, shouting, "Where is my answer?" The demon laughed and with a shrug of his shoulders, he said, "Because it's dead, you fool, because it's dead!" With that, he continued his journey, collecting berries deep in the forest.

TWO SISTERS

Rose Red lay lifeless in the heart of the forest, under the watchful eye of the spirits. Snow White was nowhere to be found, and the wicked dwarf, still alive, circled poor Rose as she lay motionless amidst the fallen leaves. She remained as still as a butterfly resting on a bed of flowers, as still as a

88

frightened mouse. Her stillness was profound, and the wicked dwarf yearned for her to be alive.

This tale unfolded on a summer's day while Snow White rested in a tree, patiently waiting for the dwarf to depart. She gently shook the blossom from the tree onto Rose's face, and in that moment, Rose blinked and twitched, returning to life. Both sisters exchanged joyful smiles and danced beneath the tree. When their dance concluded, they fled into eternity, heading toward their dreamland. As they ran, their clothing transformed into armour, and swords materialised in their hands. In every century, a girl would say, "I've seen armoured women," yet no one would believe her, and still, she would never forget.

Upon the dwarf's return, finding both sisters gone, he cursed, "Damn you! I'll see you in hell!" But he had quite a long journey ahead of him!

DOVE

Soft wing
Blue eye
Feel the softness swoop down
Onto my neck

Perhaps it sheds some blood
Drip, drip
Falling, falling
The dove is falling

Shot by a mean gun
With angry grimace

89

Poor broken wing
It aches, it hurts

The dove changed from white to red
Drip, drip
Falling, falling

Dove falls somewhere far away
Angry grimace can't find her
Shakes mean fist

The dove lies in a shallow ditch
Blood-stained earth
She takes one last breath

The dove's wing lands on bloody earth
Angry grimace gives up
Spits the ground
Leaves dove alone

Clouds floating
Lift dove towards the sky
Spirits welcome her

Broken wing
Blood washed away
It aches, it hurts
Drip, drip
Falling, falling

BUTTERFLY

The dancer stretches every part of her body until it is sore, and she cries in pain. Each day, she pirouettes and leaps so that her tutor can say, "Wonderful!" as she smokes her cigarette.

The tutor thinks she has the dancer in her power, but little does she know that each day, after rehearsals, the dancer escapes to meet a beautiful man who waits for her beside a fountain in the park.

Then, they would make love beneath the blossom trees and magnolias, entangled with the leaves and insects.
Each day, they would secretly meet like this until one day, the dancer accidentally killed a butterfly perched delicately beside her on the grass. Unusual things began to happen after that. Later, she dreamed she had made love to the butterfly by mistake.

The next day, she grew very weary. Sometimes she felt as though she was turning into a butterfly. As she had become the butterfly's killer, it seemed her tutor was now becoming her killer too.

The dance tutor would hit her with a piece of cane and tell her she wasn't concentrating.

After that, there was no more dancing. The dancer never appeared again.

Her lover came looking for her at the studio so many times that he eventually thought she had deserted him. The tutor has another prize pupil now.

Little do they know, the dancer sits by the open window, observing the world in silence. That's all she can do now with a broken wing.

RADIO CITY

Little stars, their smiles akin to riddles, gracefully unveil their heads from the abyss above. I watch them sparkle; my face bathed in their ethereal glow. Closing my eyes, tears cascade from my soul. With sealed eyes, the air grows colder, yet I sense the little stars smiling down upon me. Descending to the ground, they merge with the earth, giving rise to strange, contorted plants. Carnal green stems rise, unfurling large red petals resembling inner organs. Then, as if on some cosmic signal, the stars extinguish themselves.

"Goodbye," I murmur. "See you in Radio City."

Radio City, a surreal, digitized realm from my dreams, beckons me.

"I'm journeying there," I whisper to the stars, "to silence the radios, so every voice may echo, and peace can reign once more."

"Off I go," I declare, "to quiet the commotion."

I nestle within a flower and slip through its stem.

"Goodbye," the stars call out. "May fortune follow you," their voices echoing like cosmic whispers.

Radio City is a grey and urban, surreal place. I loathe negative spaces. It hisses like a malfunctioning radio.

At last, I locate the colossal dial that governs the city and successfully silence it. Suddenly, the hissing evaporates, and I watch with delight as tranquillity surrounds all.

THE FIGUREHEAD

"Here I am," she thought, "attached to this strange ship. They do not know that I can think and see everything that they do. Oh, the silly fools! How blind they are."

She looked around her. The dark and turbulent ocean sparkled like a vast magical potion.
"I am the leader of this ship," she thought. "I'm admired by many men and envied by many women."

Undoubtedly, she was a striking figurehead, her ebony hair cascading like feral serpents in the wind and her long, slender neck led to a beautiful torso chest and a slender waist, all contained inside a dark green corset.

Sometimes the sailors would sit and confide their troubles in her. Their wives had met someone else, or they had fallen in love with some strange lady from a distant land.

She heard many problems, but in the end, it was she they always returned to.

MY FRIEND, VIOLA

My violin hangs on the wall. Once upon a time, it was deep orange wood, and my fingers plucked each note anxiously while my teacher comforted her baby as she cried in the cot.

So many things my violin has seen. She watched me separate from my first love. She watched me prepare myself before I ventured into the town at night, searching for a soul to share my bed.

I went through many changes - then of course, so did she.

One afternoon, I delicately painted her with blue and gold, envisioning an ornate, exquisite rarity reminiscent of Versailles, a blend of pomp and the Orient. "Oh, look at that lovely violin!" people would exclaim.

As the years passed, she lost a key, then a string, until all her strings were no longer there. Eventually, she lost her bridge, and I decided she would serve as an object of admiration alone.

The saddest day came when I returned to the violin shop and inquired about the possibility of repairing her.

"All these things can be done," the man replied, "but she will never have the same tone."

Alas, now my poor violin has lost her voice. How melancholy she must feel!

Turning Point

Something happened yesterday. Something changed. "Maybe it was just me," he said.

"In what way?" I asked.

"Well, you won't know until after it happens," he replied.

I thought about that remark. What he felt had changed had not yet happened. How strange!

It's raining. Our tent gently patters with rain, and the air inside is musty and damp. The grass is fresh and green, and I feel calm to know I have become a part of nature today. My soul, for a few seconds, came and saluted me as it had many times before when I was young and free.

Here's to the peace and beauty of that field. Surround me, dear birds. Make merriment with your song and make this moment last!

The Girl Who Never Grew Up

Snow obscures the streets; rubble creates an ocean of hopelessness. One cannot recognize this town lately. If you look around, you can just see the newly built surrounding wall. The street runs through this narrow town and disappears into nowhere.

On the corner of one lane stands a young girl. She wears a white band on her right arm bearing a yellow star. She stares out at the tall men in their uniforms. Her face is thin and pale. Her shoes are smothered in rags to keep out the cold. She has only just been told why she is here, but still; she is unable to understand it all. "Why me?" she wonders.

The sky is becoming darker, and the few lamps light up the sad faces of the other people. The young girl huddles in a corner. She wonders what has happened to her other girlfriends. They never came back; but from where?

Some of the men in their uniforms remind her of the fairy-tale princes she used to dream about with their fine features and flaxen hair. She would often stand on that corner of the street begging them for food.

One day, she observed a soldier in the company of a friend, both sharing boisterous laughter as they witnessed the cruel act of an old man having his beard forcefully trimmed.

"Why did he find it funny?" thought the girl. "Princes are supposed to be good."

The old man stood there silently and didn't seem to care. "But he did really," she thought.

As the soldiers left, the prince noticed the little girl who had seen everything. She reminded him of the gipsy girl in a story his mother once told him long ago. He smiled for a second with the warm memory but then his face turned cold and showed no emotion. The little girl no longer saw him as the prince in her dreams.

As the weeks went by, the weather became colder. Rumours began to spread around that they would all be leaving soon. "Somewhere better, hopefully," thought the little girl. She saw many people disappear with the soldiers. The people carried the minimal number of belongings they owned. Many of these belongings were taken away from them as they climbed into the huge trucks. The people never knew where they were going, and no one heard from them again.

The days passed, and still, more people left. The little girl clutched her coat tightly. If only she knew where her mother and brother were. She began to feel incredibly alone. Often, the girl had wondered why she was not allowed outside this small piece of town. The soldiers always drove away, but she did not know where.

One day the little girl became ill. She had hardly eaten for weeks; just thin soup. At one point, she, and the people she was surrounded by had received parcels from friends and relatives with food inside, but now, that had suddenly stopped. Each day, someone became very sick in the small town. The people became slower and fewer. She remembered the happy days at home with her family: the laughter, the friendly faces, and the dreams she had always had. They didn't match up to this desolate, lonely place.

One day the little girl was lined up with many other children. She was told she was going somewhere better, but she didn't trust them. She held the hand of a younger girl who was crying. Why is there no room for us to sit down, she thought. How will I breathe? How will I use the toilet?

After three days of travelling with no food, they were finally let out. She breathed in the fresh air, and it seemed like she might die of exhaustion. As she looked around, she saw trees, and it felt like the entire journey had been worth it just to see trees again.

The soldiers lined her up with the others. She recognized one of the soldiers; the one who had cut off the old man's beard, the one she used to think was her prince. He looked at her. His face was thinner, and his eyes appeared empty. The little girl thought he looked so sad, and she wanted to comfort him, to tell him that everything would be alright and that he was still her handsome prince. But his look frightened her. Any warmth had vanished.

There was the sound of screams and bullets. The soldiers left the misty green field in silence, but some started to laugh. Some became quite forthright and business-like, organizing the closing of the truck doors efficiently. The soldier with the flaxen hair looked at the ground. He felt faint and lifeless. He kicked the mud, allowing it to douse his boots and his clothes, and then he secretly covered his face with the cool wet earth as if to remind himself he was still real.

"Is this who I've become?" he murmured. "I despise myself," and with those words, he climbed back into the truck, leaving the receding trees and the little girl, forever frozen in time, to fade in the distance.

FIRST THOUGHT ON A HILL

Incredible things can exist, like this moment on a hill. A mysterious path before me, a fissure in the distant mountain. Emeralds and sapphires surround me, and ochre yellow recedes in patches throughout the distant trees. Could I be more elated than I am right now, surrounded by dandelions and a brilliant ray of light seeping through a shimmering salmon cloud?

At this moment, I am filled with joy, and my heart is uplifted by the hopes of dreams that have not yet transpired. Yes, it's all still possible. Suddenly, everything comes to life once more. I could dance! I could dance! I could cry for all of life's pains, but no, I can't because up here, there is only hope and happiness.

I feel like a faint echo in this heavenly wilderness. Suddenly, it seems strange that we move, while everything else stands still. All the motion I see is a gentle rustle of grass and thistles in the breeze and the sunlight twinkling on the winding streams.

Ancient walls wind throughout the fields. What is it that makes us feel so alone? Quite often, it's because nature turns its back on us and no longer welcomes us into its beautiful abundance. And when you feel abandoned by nature, nothing matters anymore. All is lost.

SECOND THOUGHT ON A HILL

Why must we harbour enemies? Anger courses through our veins, a turbulent force restraining our freedom. "Leave my mind! Let us revel in happiness and embrace one another with love. Love me, please. I crave love. We all yearn for love."

A pearly cloud weaves its way from behind the mountain. Twelve birds are touched by the blessing of flight as they gracefully soar across this timeless glade of beauty. Their descent is a dance, synchronizing with the rhythm of my own heart. They bestow upon my strength. Who would have imagined that twelve birds could breathe life back into me?

CLOUDS

A seahorse transpired through an icy blue cloud, its head tilting into a salmon bow. It drifted and slanted into the void, leaving only a shadowy trace of its existence. Two joyful dolphins leapt through the air, one transforming into a horse while the other remained melancholy. A monstrous creature jumped from a cliff, crying out, "We have not died yet!" Suddenly, it withered once more, grasping at its final chance for existence before transforming into a lizard ghost. A wild, dark boar guided it far away. An eye gazed down at me, as real as could be. It drew closer and closer, then blinked into obscurity to reveal a brighter ray behind. All clouds dissipated, except for a large flying rat, not a ram. It receded, fading until it vanished. All was grey until a leaping dog nipped at a cloud. In the distance, a ship sailed far away on a distant sea.

THE END

The enchanting soul continues to meander down the road, beaming at passers-by, and offering her hat in greeting to the sun. She twirls with the birds, and the sun's radiant beams gently elevate her above the earth. The rain takes on a gilded hue, showering down upon the town, transforming the buildings into ornate sculptures and the townsfolk into enchanted statues.

The soul becomes entranced in a mist of golden light, as she tilts her head to the ethereal breeze. In this mystical moment, only the sensation of golden raindrops caressing her face and the breeze murmuring like a magical veil matter. This wondrous veil connects her, in part, to the suburban street with its enchanted trees, buildings, and people, and, in part, to the celestial sky, where the planets above glisten in golden radiance, and thoughts are eternally imbued with enchantment.

One ethereal soul continues her journey, understanding that she is forever free.

**In this collection of fairy tales, every story holds a valuable lesson.
Below is a list of the morals found in each tale.**

The Dance
*Embrace the allure of the unknown journey, finding joy in exploring uncharted
territories despite uncertainty, unveiling the wonders of the unfamiliar.*

Secrets of the Forest
*Delving into risk and desire, it portrays the allure of the unknown, intertwining
compassion and self-discovery in life's transformative journey.*

The Red Bride
*In her red wedding attire, the bride escapes societal chains, embracing freedom
through nature's elements in her transformative journey.*

The Princess in the Pond
*Life's intricate choices and the quest for happiness are showcased, emphasising
freedom amid sacrifices and the enigmatic outcomes of decisions.*

The Flower of Goodness
*Life's cyclical journey and self-discovery are spotlighted, advocating the embrace
of uncertainty for profound self-realisation and purpose. It explores
interconnectedness, revealing vulnerability's transformative potential and an
enriched view of life's beauty.*

Familiar Places
*The story highlights finding peace in solitude, accepting change, and cherishing
memories. It emphasises the bittersweetness of life's fleeting moments, the power of
introspection, and the tranquillity found in reconnecting with nature.*

The Things We Do for Love
The moral of this story.
*Envy's bitter touch estranges kinship; only valour and enduring love can conquer
the darkest of destinies.*

China Flowers
*One could interpret this story as an exploration of the complexities of desire and
disillusionment, woven within the fabric of mundane existence. The tale
encapsulates the maiden's yearning for a romanticised life, symbolised by her
desires for luxurious possessions and an idyllic experience.*

Autumn
*The moral of this story appears to revolve around the longing for escapism and the
transient nature of desires. It delves into the allure of fantasy to escape the*

mundane, suggesting that even fleeting moments of enchantment, though temporary, can deeply impact one's perception and memory.

Ice
The story grapples with the struggle between the safety of the familiar and the allure of the unknown, highlighting the quest for balance and the potential isolation that comes with choosing safety over freedom.

Another Day
The story's moral: Nature's rejuvenation offers solace, inviting a return to innocent joy. Embrace life's carefree aspects, finding peace through immersion in the natural world.

Frosty Morning
In a cold world, human connections combat fear and loneliness, illustrating kindness as a shield against desolation and emphasising the power of relationships in fostering warmth and empathy.

Bliss
The story underscores the elusive nature of happiness, imprisoned within unfulfilled desires and haunting obsessions. It speaks of missed opportunities and the yearning for liberation from the burdens that confine one's joy, ultimately longing for the freedom to rediscover true bliss.

Chandeliers
The story underscores the complexity of emotions, portraying the struggle of concealing personal sorrow behind a facade. It urges deeper connections beyond surface appearances, emphasising the significance of authenticity in expressing true emotions rather than hiding behind masks.

The Wound
The story emphasises healing from past trauma for inner peace. It contrasts a peaceful present with a turbulent past, symbolised by the encounter between red and yellow horses. The red horse's bleeding wound in the sky signifies the impact of unresolved trauma, urging the need to address emotional wounds for peace and healing.

The Witch with A Tear in The Corner of Her Eye
The story reflects the introspective journey of self-realisation and the quest for purpose, illustrating the cyclical nature of searching for meaning amidst a sense of existential detachment and longing for genuine connection.

The Carousel
Finding solace in unexpected places, the carousel represents joy and cherished memories. Its appearance amidst despair hints at the persistence of unexpected sources of comfort and wonder, illuminating hope even in the darkest times.

Angel
This tale warns against self-sacrifice for others, revealing the perils of absolute trust and neglecting personal well-being. It depicts how excessive selflessness can lead to personal devastation and abandonment.

The Glass Door
The moral of this story is that seeking validation or trying to change oneself to fit others' expectations can lead to losing one's true uniqueness and happiness.

The Queen and her Angry Spirit
The story highlights unchecked anger's impact, showcasing the Queen's evolution after betrayal: mastering wisdom over anger, valuing empathy, and advocating for balanced emotional responses, urging a measured approach to anger and retribution.

Anna's well
The story's moral stresses the consequences of deceit and the vital importance of honesty, responsibility, and addressing problems rather than evading them. It emphasises the enduring power of kindness and the need for accountability and prompt action during challenging times.

The Stag Lady
The tale conveys identity's complexity via the Lady's introspection and changing self-perception. Her mirror scrutiny signifies self-understanding, culminating in a majestic stag's transformation, symbolising a deep connection to nature and a redefined self.

The Kiss
Life's fleeting moments, chance encounters, and spontaneity evoke lasting feelings, emphasising the beauty of seizing serendipitous experiences and cherishing brief but impactful memories for a timeless impact.

Mexico
Mexico's allure captivates through cultural richness and enchanting encounters, emphasising nostalgic impressions of landscapes, traditions, and people. Memories hold a hypnotic power, drawing one back into their vivid embrace like an enchanting spell.

The Music Room
The moral of this story celebrates the transformative power of music and artistic expression. It emphasises the deep connection between individuals and their art forms, portraying how music intertwines with their essence.

The Tree

The tale conveys the bond between nature and human life, symbolised by the wise tree. Its impending destruction highlights the consequence of human desires over nature's sanctity.

The Landlord
The moral of the story emphasises missed opportunities and the regret of not connecting with someone when the chance was present. It highlights the significance of seizing the moment and fostering relationships before it's too late.

Mole
The moral of the story emphasises the importance of empathy, even in the face of insignificance there is a concern for nature and creatures like the mole. It underscores the idea that even the smallest beings deserve freedom and dignity in their existence.

Even Though
The narrative underscores the regret that arises from not having closure or the opportunity to convey feelings, urging one to appreciate and embrace moments as they occur, without leaving sentiments unspoken or gestures unmade.

The Swan
The story illustrates the ramifications of unrequited love and the yearning for a lost connection across different planes of existence. It delves into an enigma, blurring the boundaries between dreams and reality, hinting at desires persisting beyond waking life's limits.

Walking in the Sky
The tale yearns for liberation from routine, weaving nature and fantasy, signifying time's passage and innocence's loss via the lost crown, illustrating life's unpredictable journey and the splintering of dreams.

The Stream
The tale highlights the deep bond between nature and emotions, portraying how natural elements influence thoughts and dreams. It symbolises the fusion of human resilience with nature's enduring traits, stressing the vital acknowledgement of our inherent connection to the natural world.

Firefly
The story illustrates emotions' fleeting nature, showcasing shifts from anger to emptiness, capturing life's unpredictability, and emphasising the need to navigate through diverse feelings and circumstances.

Knights of the Sword
The moral of the story conveys the enduring cycle of conflict and violence, painting a vivid picture of the eternal nature of human struggles and warfare. It highlights the relentless passage of time amid brutality, symbolised by the interplay of ice, blood, and nature's tranquility against the backdrop of relentless battles.

The Wife of Brighton
The tale's moral hints at embracing death's inevitability with readiness, showcasing the protagonist's peaceful acceptance and preparedness for the end. It underscores finding comfort in life's experiences, leading to a serene outlook towards the finality of existence.

Red Polish
The tale portrays societal pressure to conform, reflecting biases against individuality. Rejecting red nail polish symbolises the struggle for acceptance amidst societal norms, underscoring challenges faced when deviating from standards.

Jigsaw
Understanding someone fully is akin to solving a puzzle, highlighting the complexity and desire for genuine comprehension in relationships, while acknowledging the cyclic nature of understanding amid moments of turmoil and reconstruction.

Time to Laugh
The story's moral: Life's genuine moments of joy, even if fleeting and transient, offer profound connections and authenticity, despite the facade of normalcy or pretence.

Green Chair
The story's moral is that objects may hold a transformative power, reflecting inner emotions and experiences. It explores the chair's symbolic significance, embodying introspection, the changing nature of emotions, and the deep connection between tangible objects and one's internal journey.

The Mermaid's Tail
The tale challenges traditional narratives, blending surrealism and postmodern themes to question conventional moral teachings. It navigates the realms of desire, danger, and transformation, inviting contemplation beyond typical moral conclusions.

Ghost
The moral of the ghost story is about the enduring bond between a father and his lost daughter, symbolising the struggle to let go and find closure after a tragic loss. It highlights the haunting nature of grief, where the father's longing and memories keep his daughter's spirit alive, yet he cannot reach her, signifying the inability to fully move on from the past.

Reflections
Rita's transformations and the idea of eating her reflection or identity can symbolise the consumption or loss of her sense of self, leading to consequences and a loss of identity. It's a symbolic representation of the repercussions of losing or compromising one's essence or individuality.

The Witch
A tale cautioning against idealising illusions, it warns of disillusionment when faced with reality. It speaks of the repercussions of rejecting truth and attempting to manipulate reality to fit desires, resulting in enduring sorrow and regret.

Beneath the Earth
The story implies the allure of an ethereal world beneath ours, where love transcends reality's boundaries. It portrays the possibility of an eternal union, transcending time and space, a realm where lovers find everlasting rest amid enchanting landscapes and celestial beauty.

The Burial
Ignoring warnings risks unforeseen dangers, echoing the importance of heeding advice. The tale underlines the consequences of disregarding caution, showcasing a shift from indifference to empathy. Compassion's value emerges as the protagonist learns from disregarding intuition, emphasising the repercussions of neglecting premonitions.

The Dinner
The story underscores the veneer of conviviality concealing hidden tensions and suppressed emotions. It epitomises the dichotomy between laughter and silence, depicting the struggle to bridge disparate worlds within human interactions.

The Demon
The demon's final task of burning the tree symbolises the inevitability of destruction when someone refuses to acknowledge the truth. The story highlights the importance of honesty, accountability, and understanding the consequences of one's choices, revealing that denying reality only leads to eventual harm and loss.

Two Sisters
"Two Sisters" contrasts vulnerability with resilience; the dwarf's malevolence falls against the sisters' empowerment, symbolising triumph over adversity. Nature's revival underscores the power of resilience, leading to the sisters' eventual freedom.

Dove
The poem "DOVE" depicts a dove's tragic demise, transitioning from innocence to a sorrowful end, symbolising the loss of peace and the cruelty of human actions.

Butterfly
The moral of this dark fairy tale cautions about the consequences of actions and the interconnectedness of life. It highlights the fragility of existence and how inadvertently harming even the smallest creature can lead to a series of unsettling events. The story reflects the theme of guilt and how one's actions can spiral into personal anguish and loss.

Radio City
The story follows a protagonist's mission to silence the turmoil in Radio City, highlighting personal agency in restoring peace amid chaos. It illustrates the transformative power of determined actions in bringing tranquillity to a dissonant environment.

The Figurehead
The moral of this story suggests the power of observation and empathy, portraying the protagonist's silent understanding and comforting presence among the ship's crew. It reflects how despite seeking solace elsewhere, people often find reassurance in familiar and steadfast sources of support.

My Friend, Viola
The violin symbolises the passage of time and irreversible change, losing its essence despite attempts at restoration. Its silence echoes the sentimental value of treasured possessions amidst the inevitability of transformation.

Turning Point
The moral of "Turning Point" reflects the significance of embracing moments of change and appreciating the simple, serene beauty of nature. It underscores the importance of being present now and finding solace in the tranquillity of nature amid life's transitions.

The Girl Who Never Grew Up
The moral of this dark fairy tale seems to convey the devastating consequences of indifference, cruelty, and the moral decay resulting from societal indifference and inhumanity. It touches on the erosion of compassion, the harrowing impact of war and totalitarianism, and the loss of innocence amidst an unforgiving and brutal world.

First Thought on a Hill
Nature's serene beauty uplifts spirits, offering hope and joy amidst life's challenges. However, feeling abandoned by nature brings a sense of isolation and loss, emphasising our deep connection to the natural world for fulfilment.

Second Thought on a Hill
The moral of "Second Thought on a Hill" is about the transformative power of love and the renewal it brings, symbolised by the birds' flight and the restoration of inner strength through connection and compassion.

Clouds
Overall, these symbolic elements represent a variety of themes such as change, transformation, resilience, awareness, freedom, and the unpredictability of life's journey. However, as the symbolism is abstract and open-ended, the interpretation can vary widely based on individual perspectives and contexts.

The End

The moral of this story conveys the essence of freedom and the connection between the ethereal and the earthly. It speaks of embracing enchantment and finding freedom in the harmonious connection between oneself and the mystical aspects of the world. The soul's journey signifies the understanding that true freedom comes from embracing the magical elements around us and within us, allowing oneself to transcend earthly confines and become part of the eternal enchantment of the universe.

Milton Keynes UK
Ingram Content Group UK Ltd.
UKHW012249260224
438492UK00005B/319